AN URGE FOR JUSTICE

by the same author

WHO GOES NEXT?
THE BASTARD
POOL OF TEARS
A NEST OF RATS
DO NOTHIN' TILL YOU HEAR FROM ME
THE DAY OF THE PEPPERCORN KILL
THE JURY PEOPLE
THIEF OF TIME
DEATH CERTIFICATE
A RIPPLE OF MURDERS
BRAINWASH
DUTY ELSEWHERE
TAKE MURDER...
THE EYE OF THE BEHOLDER
THE VENUS FLY-TRAP
DOMINOES
MAN OF LAW
ALL ON A SUMMER'S DAY
BLAYDE R.I.P.

way
AN URGE FOR JUSTICE

John Wainwright

ST. MARTIN'S PRESS
NEW YORK

AN URGE FOR JUSTICE. Copyright © 1981 by John and Avis Wainwright. All rights reserved. Printed in the United States of America. No part of this book may be used or reproduced in any manner whatsoever without written permission except in the case of brief quotations embodied in critical articles or reviews. For information, address St. Martin's Press, 175 Fifth Avenue, New York, N.Y. 10010.

Library of Congress Cataloging in Publication Data

Wainwright, John William, 1921-
   An urge for justice.

   I. Title.
PR6073.A354U7   1982   823'.914   82-5757
ISBN 0-312-83527-2   AACR2

First published in Great Britain by Macmillan London Limited.

First U.S. Edition

10 9 8 7 6 5 4 3 2 1

For, as thou urgest justice, be assur'd
Thou shalt have justice, more than thou desir'st.

The Merchant of Venice Act IV, scene i

PROLOGUE

ONE

It began...
 Who can say with certainty where, and when, *anything* began? There must *be* a beginning. Logic insists that everything must have a beginning. And yet, perhaps, not just *one* beginning. Like the branches of a tree converging into a single trunk, it is possible that there are many beginnings... to everything.

Perhaps it began on the thirtieth of January, 1933; the day on which a one-time corporal in the Germany Army rabble-roused his way to the chancellorship of The Fatherland. Perhaps it began as long ago as that.

On the other hand, perhaps Hitler was not to blame. Perhaps Hitler was manipulated more than he ever knew.

If so, a bespectacled ex-schoolmaster and his wild theories of 'master-race' politics might be the starting point. Certainly Heinrich Himmler is a factor to be reckoned with. If not the actual 'beginning' a human 'booster station' not too far along the route.

Or Goebbels, who raised propaganda to a fine art. Or Goering, who carried self-delusion to the point of lunacy. Or Ribbentrop or Bormann or Hess... or each and all of them. When a great nation topples into the abyss of communal madness, anything can happen and a hundred thousand tiny tragedies can be triggered off; there can be a hundred thousand 'beginnings'.

But, for the sake of tidiness, a teller of tales must pinpoint a single 'beginning'. Therefore — and for the sake of tidiness — we will begin with the crime. *One* of the crimes... and merely for the sake of tidiness.

'CRIME'

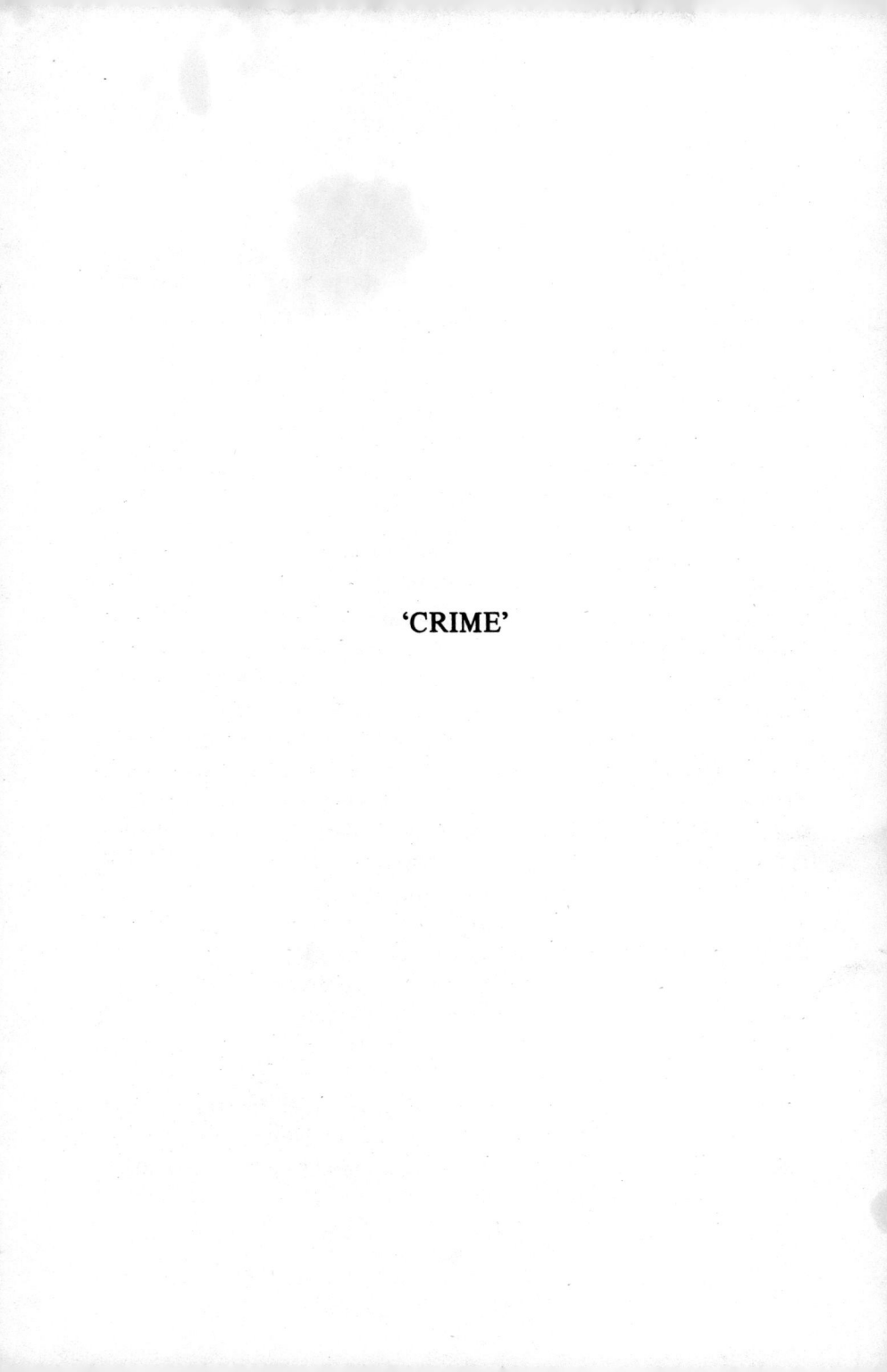

ONE

The milk-roundsman triggered off the enquiry. A previous day's untouched bottle of milk left on a doorstep might give rise to a look of mild surprise, two such bottles might cause tentative enquiries from available neighbours, but when the number reached three and the only sign of disturbance was ragged edges where blue-tits had pecked a way through the thin metal of the tops, it was time to mention the matter to the police.

It was a nice morning; a Sunday morning — Sunday, October 19th — with the clean bite of autumn frost in the air. Bill Harper had been bustling his way through the early chores at his own smallholding, loading the float with crates of bottles, cartons of eggs and the limited number of half-pint bottles of cream ordered by customers the day before. He might not have used the expression, but he was 'proving himself'. Time was he'd been one of the local bloods; boozing with a small crowd of his cronies, drunk most nights of the week, ready for a set-to with anybody who happened to cross his path. That, little more than three years ago. Then he'd met Mary and it had been a little like running into a brick wall. Six months after meeting her he'd married her . . . having made certain solemn promises. His father, owner of more acres than most in the district, had poured blunt, Yorkshire contempt on the promises. 'Tha'll no'an do it, lad. It isn't in thee.' Well, now he knew. Now they *all* knew. For Mary and young Billy he was prepared to work his balls off. A smallholding, plus a milk round covering Rimstone and all the surrounding villages and hamlets; seven days a week, from dawn till dusk and, so far, never a holiday. No boozing, no smoking; just graft . . . and a wife and a son for whom he'd happily give his life's blood.

Instead of adding to the number of milk bottles, he stepped back from the house and looked up at the windows. None of the curtains were closed. No smoke came from the chimney. Never a beautiful house, it looked less lovely than ever; the brickwork pock-marked with age and weather; the paintwork cracked and, in places, starting to peel. With a good owner — with money spent on it — it could have been given a stark dignity but, as it was, the appearance was that of decay and neglect.

'Isn't she about?'

Bill Harper turned. Mr Jessell was at the gate. He was an accountant and worked in partnership with Mr Holmes at Bordfield. Mr Holmes owned the first house on the left at the mouth of the cul-de-sac and, in order to save petrol, they usually travelled to the office in the one car, week about. They, too, often used Sunday mornings as a means of catching up with the back-log. Being your own boss had its advantages . . . it also had a hell of a lot of *dis*advantages.

Harper walked to the gate, glancing back at the house as he did so.

He said, 'There's three days' milk on the step.'

'Oh!'

'I think we should tell somebody.'

'She might be ill,' contributed Jessell. 'She's getting on a bit.'

'Unless she's on holiday.'

'I haven't heard anything. They usually know.'

'They?'

'The womenfolk. They usually know. They usually mention things.'

'She didn't cancel her milk,' said Harper.

'She might be ill,' repeated Jessell.

'Er — Constable Stone?' Harper frowned, as if unwilling to commit himself unreservedly.

Jessell said, 'I'll nip back home and phone him.'

'Aye.' Harper nodded. 'I'll deliver to the other houses . . . then wait.'

Sammy Stone. Full style and title, Police Constable 1781 Samuel Henry Stone. Responsible (along with Wilf Pinter) for the policing of Rimstone Beat; which was an 'outside' or 'detached' beat, and part of Sopworth Section; which, in turn, was part of Beechwood Brook Division; which, in turn, was part of Bordfield Region; which, in turn, was part of Lessford Metropolitan Police District . . . and so on *ad infinitum*!

A very unimportant 'patch'; a mere brush-stroke in the grand design of law-enforcement.

Not that Sammy Stone worried overmuch about such trivialities.

A little less than five years to go to Pension Day. Not a hope in hell of ever making sergeant . . . or wanting to. Well and truly married, with one son and one daughter. The son away at Durham University, working for his Finals and a degree in some obscure branch of Sociology. ('He can't unknot his own bloody life. He'll be a bonny bugger to advise other people.') His daughter married and living in Salford ('I've kept her long enough. Now let some other silly sod keep her.') He'd bobbied some of the roughest spots in the old Lessford City Force. And, when that useless nerk, Karn, had filled his hole full and been given the big E — when Rimstone Beat had become light one village bobby — and he, Sammy Stone, had been offered the transfer, he'd nearly snatched their hand off. Money for old rope! And Wilf Pinter (despite his missus having kicked the bucket only recently) was a good lad to share the harness; a bit on the solemn side — not quite the life and soul of any party — but, above all else, no skiver. All in all, the best move he'd made in his whole police career . . . if you could call it a career.

As he lumbered down the stairs to the telephone in the hall of the police house, he unbuttoned the jacket of his pyjamas and scratched his not inconsiderable belly. He'd been on duty till two o'clock that morning and now it wasn't much past seven, and five hours could hardly be called 'a good night's sleep'. Ah, well, that's what being a village bobby boiled down to. On tap twenty-four hours a day, and old Wilf was up to the eyeballs with a Motor Manslaughter job. It was his 'catch' and he wasn't grumbling.

Still scratching his belly with one hand, he yawned, picked up the receiver and said, 'Constable Stone, here.'

It really was an ugly looking house. The cul-de-sac consisted of eleven houses — five on each side and one at the far end — each standing in its own grounds and, if the truth be told, none of them a treat for the eye. Each had its own unsightly features but, as far as the other ten were concerned, paint, a tidy garden, an occasional picture window (that sort of thing) had done much to counter the brooding quality. But this one — Number Five and third house up on the left — stood there beyond its untrimmed hedge, surrounded by weed-infested garden and was by far the ugliest. Stone's mini-van was parked behind Harper's milk-float. Holmes had joined Jessell and the four men gazed at the huge, squalid house from the slightly drunken gate.

'Knocked, have you?' asked Stone.

'Er — no — not yet.' Harper felt strangely guilty — and a little stupid — as he answered the question.

'We'd better knock.'

Stone lumbered down the broken path, towards the front door. From the rear he looked almost unbelievably wide as the unbuttoned sports jacket he'd slipped on over his uniform trousers and shirt flapped about his hips. Naked on the bathroom scales he topped the sixteen stone mark and yet, like so many large men, he was surprisingly light on his feet. The lumbering effect was produced by the sway of his immense trunk, supported by thick thighs but, when necessary, he could move and pounce with the uncoiled-spring speed of a jungle cat . . . as some of the less lawful residents of Lessford City had found to their cost.

He balled a fist and, using it like a hammer, thudded on the panels of the front door. A few flakes of paint fell from the surface of the door. Other than that, nothing. He waited, then hammered a second time. Still nothing. He turned and rejoined the three men at the gate.

'Thursday, Friday and yesterday's milk?'

Harper nodded.

'You didn't think to kick up a stink sooner?'

Harper opened his mouth, as if to say something, then closed it and remained silent.

'Anybody seen her recently?' asked Stone.

Jessell said, 'I haven't.'

Holmes said, 'No . . . but I rarely do see her.'

'Lights in the windows, after dark?'

Jessell shook his head.

Holmes said, 'I don't often pass the house.'

'Right.' Stone buttoned his jacket. 'We'd better have a look round. Try the ground floor windows as you pass.'

Indian file fashion, they walked up the path. Stone and Harper turned left at the front door. Jessell and Holmes turned right. Each pair half-circled the house, trying windows, shielding their eyes and trying to penetrate the gloom of unlit rooms and grimy glass. They met and grouped at the rear door, where Stone once again pounded the woodwork without effect.

'Summat's up,' said Harper sadly.

'Summat,' agreed Stone. Then pointedly, 'I think I smell gas.'

Holmes sniffed and said, 'I have a good sense of smell, but I can't . . .'

'Just in case,' said Stone heavily. 'It gives me a reason for breaking in.'

'Oh — ah — yes.' A watery smile flickered across Holmes's lips. 'On second thoughts. Now you come to mention it.'

Jessell was a little disappointed. He was a TV cops-and-robbers enthusiast. He expected to see a hunk of British Constabulary hurl itself at the rear door. Stone, on the other hand, valued his shoulder-blade and collar bone. He sought an ancient brick from among the debris of the garden, then gently — almost fastidiously — tapped all the glass from a frame of the panelled sidepieces alongside the door. He took his time. He removed every tiny piece of glass. Then he slipped off his jacket, handed it to Jessell and threaded his arm carefully through the opening. There was a moment of feeling and fumbling, then the three watching men heard a latch-lock turn and snap into an 'open' position. With his free hand Stone turned the door knob, but the door remained fastened. Stone muttered 'Damn!' then contorted himself until his side was hard against the panels, stood on his toes and reached high. The waiting men heard a bolt being slipped from its socket. Stone pulled his arm from the hole, turned the knob of the door and pushed, hard. The door 'gave' a little, but the base remained firm.

Stone said, 'There's a bolt at the bottom and I can't reach it. If it's like the one at the top, it won't take much shifting.'

He turned his back to the door, settled his shoulders squarely against the woodwork, then put a hand behind his back and twisted the knob. He heaved himself backwards and, at the same time, slammed the heel of his left foot against the base of the door. The wood splintered and Stone staggered backwards and grabbed the upright of the door frame to stop himself from sprawling.

And now there was a way into this gloomy house the three men, Harper, Jessell and Holmes, hung back and seemed unwilling to enter.

The relief showed on their faces when Stone said, 'You three stay here. I'll let you know.'

The broken door led into a large porch and a second door (which was unlocked) led from the porch to a huge kitchen. There was a rank and foetid smell about the kitchen; unwashed crockery, scraps of half-eaten food and mouse droppings scattered the surface of a large, plain deal-topped table; the floor was covered with cheap, worn lino; an ugly, unpolished 'Yorkist' range held dead ashes and on both sides of the chimney breast double-doored kitchen cupboards were fixed to the wall. Apart from the table, the only other furniture was an assortment of unmatching kitchen chairs (four of them) and a massive mahogany sideboard, chipped and scratched and with an odd collection of crockery and a cheap vase holding dead flowers placed, without pattern, upon its top.

The door leading from the kitchen was ajar. Sammy Stone stared at it and scowled. Some sixth sense, something not too far removed from ESP and something which had grown and matured throughout a small lifetime of 'gut' policing, warned him that beyond that door was . . . something. Specifics, in such cases, are unimportant. Only the knowledge — the absolute certainty — matters. Somebody waiting to clobber him, perhaps. Something dangerous. Something horrific.

The door opened outwards from the kitchen. To open it, in the normal way, was to step beyond it. Therefore, Stone didn't open it in the normal way.

He moved cautiously across the lino of the kitchen. Softly; so softly that he could hear the hurried scrape and scurry as vermin — mice and perhaps rats — sought safer shelter. When he was about a yard from the door he halted. Tensed himself for action; became ready to explode either left or right, or even ahead and through the door, should circumstances call for such action. Then he raised his right foot, bent his knee and slammed the flat underside of his shoe against the face of the door, alongside the knob.

The door flew open, banged against the wall of the short passage leading to the hall, rebounded a few inches, then quivered.

The woman was in the hall.

The floor of the hall was tiled. Red tiles which, when polished, cause mats and rugs to skate and bring the unwary flat on their backs. But the tiles hadn't been polished for years. As Stone looked along the passage a banistered staircase rose to the floor above on his right; it started in the hall — at one side of the hall — and rose towards the door leading to the kitchen. The walls of the hall were colour-washed in what looked to be cheap emulsion paint; a dark stone shade and patchy, either from dampness or bad, amateur application. On Stone's left (as he looked up the passage and into the hall) there was a door which, obviously, led into one of the front rooms; it was some distance from him and almost a right-hand turn to anybody entering the front of the house. Nearer to him, not much more than a foot from the door leading to the front room, was a row of six clothes pegs. Not hooks; stout wooden pegs let into a thick base; the sort of clothes pegs found in cloakrooms and foyers of chapels.

Six such pegs and (counting from Stone's end of the row) the woman was hanging from the fifth peg.

Her feet were tied. Her hands were tied behind her back. The wire which looped her neck and suspended her from the peg had bitten into the flesh and the trickle of blood had congealed and turned black. Her eyes bulged and stared, sightlessly, at the rails and banister of the stairs. Her tongue protruded from her gaping mouth. Her face was mottled puce and purple. The violence with which Stone had kicked open the door had caused her to swing gently, and had sent the few out-of-season flies spiralling and buzzing from where they'd been gorging themselves.

TWO

Tallboy. Christopher 'Chris' Tallboy. *Chief Superintendent* Tallboy. The local supremo of Beechwood Brook Division. It could be said he'd seen it all. Muck and filth by the middenful. Foulness almost beyond belief. Enough twisted mentalities to fill a dozen Bedlams.

This, of course, was not to be wondered at; a score of senior policemen in every force of the U.K. could have made the same sorry claim. It went with the job; the rottenness and the disgust; the unsavouriness and the rancidness. The near-belief that man's inhumanity to man knows no bounds. That sheer, naked evil is the life-spring of half the world's population.

The wonder was that these men retained a belief in the goodness of the other half.

With Tallboy (as with many) it was like closing a door in the mind. The dead woman's body was a fact; it was there to be seen and, because it was there, somebody had placed it there. A fact, therefore, but a fact to be placed firmly beyond that mental door.

Tallboy, moreover, was having to adjust to a new life-style. Not since he'd been a young constable, pounding paving-stones and escorting old ladies across busy streets, had he worn a uniform. From detective constable he'd moved up the ranks within the heady atmosphere of the C.I.D. Up to, and including, detective chief inspector. Sure, he'd known all about the vicissitudes of the uniformed branch; known that whereas he and his colleagues could concentrate their attention upon the clobbering of villans, his buddies in uniform had less flamboyant (but equally important) duties to perform.

Well, now he *really* knew.

On one day of particularly wild activity certain coming and goings had triggered off a thought within the mind of Assistant Chief Constable (Crime) Harris and, as a result, Chris Tallboy had done a double shuffle, flipped past one rung of the promotion ladder and ended up as chief superintendent, in uniform and Beechwood Brook Divisional Officer.*

Very nice, too. Especially in view of the fact that his late father-in-law, Charles Ripley, had once occupied that same chair. When he'd broken the news to his wife, Susan, she'd wept a little. Memories, pride. Probably a touch of sorrow, probably a hint of trepidation, because Susan knew (as Chris Tallboy knew) that Beechwood Brook had damn near broken a good marriage. It was one hell of a division, both in size and in content and, as such, it demanded far more attention than any mistress.

One more thing which tended to give Tallboy waking nightmares. Charles Ripley had 'made' Beechwood Brook; he'd given it a peculiar stamp. A 'feel' like no other division in the force. And after Ripley, Blayde (Detective Chief Superintendent Robert Blayde, present Head of Bordfield Region C.I.D.) had added *his* mark in the few months he'd held the reins. That Blakey had followed Blayde, and that Blakey had been less than a pale shadow of his two predecessors, mattered little. The magic had been far too deep for Blakey to shift. It was still 'Ripley's Division' . . . always would be. And the impression was that Ripley's ghost hovered around, ever critical and never quite satisfied.

Tallboy, Detective Sergeant Kelly and Police Constable Stone stood at the door of the kitchen, looked towards the hall and viewed the woman's hanging body. They were good coppers. Practical coppers. They all knew the wisdom of doing nothing until you knew *exactly* what you were going to do. They kept their hands firmly in the pockets of their trousers.

'Touch anything?' Tallboy asked the question. He could have guessed the answer, but the question had to be asked.

'The outside door knob,' Stone moved his head. 'I kicked that door open. Other than that, nothing.'

'Anne Miller,' mused Tallboy. 'What do we know?'

'Not a lot.' Stone didn't waste time excusing himself. 'I'd never met her. From what the three outside say, a bit of a recluse. Unmarried . . . maybe divorced, maybe a widow. Whatever, no man

---

*All on a Summer's Day by John Wainwright, Macmillan, 1981.

about the house. Other than that.' He moved his shoulders. 'She didn't take her milk in Thursday, Friday and yesterday.'

Kelly said, 'I've sent Harper on his way, to finish his round. He'll be at home for a statement this evening.'

Tallboy nodded his agreement.

For a moment he stood and kept dark thoughts to himself. Thoughts which revolved around a single question. 'How many more times?' How many more brutalised bodies had he yet to view? How many more murder enquiries had he to either be involved in or (as now) actually trigger off? How many more sleepless nights? How many more mealless days? How many more 'interviews'? How many more snivelling bastards making piffling excuses for the inexcusable?

He sighed and said, 'Those two outside . . .'

'Jessell and Holmes,' contributed Stone. 'They're neighbours.'

'Arrange for them to be seen later. Statements . . . and from their wives and families. The usual thing.'

'Yes, sir.'

Stone turned and left the kitchen. Left the house. He wasn't sorry to go. He'd seen death enough times – in enough forms – to be beyond other than objective. But this . . . And to a harmless old lady!

In the kitchen Tallboy and Kelly stood, unmoving and silent, for a few moments.

Then Tallboy said, 'We'll seal the whole cul-de-sac off. I'll contact Inspector Rowe. Arrange things.'

'Yes, sir.'

(She hadn't been the best housekeeper in the world; that minor point had been obvious, the moment they'd stepped across the threshold.)

'Chief Superintendent Blayde shouldn't be long. He'll organise the C.I.D. side of things.'

'Yes, sir.'

(Nobody – *nobody* – deserved to go this way! And on the face of things the poor bitch had been hanging there for three days.)

'It's a village. That helps. Nosey parkers . . . they see things. Not much happens they don't notice.'

'It helps,' agreed Kelly.

'We'll have Pinter out. He's been here longer than Stone. He'll have more local knowledge.'

'And Kyle?'

'Yeah . . . and Kyle.'

Kyle worked Upper Neck Beat — the neighbouring beat to Rimstone — and very often the two beats were worked 'double'. Kyle was a damn good copper; what he didn't know about Upper Neck wasn't worth knowing, nor was he a slouch as far as Rimstone was concerned. Pinter and Kyle. Between them they should know *something*.

'We'll wait outside.'

They left the house. They were careful where they trod; they kept to the broken flagstones of the path. The weeds, the brambles, the soft earth of the garden might give up some pointers when subjected to an organised search.

Thus, a murder hunt was on the way. No tyre-screaming cars. No red-necked jacks shouting and bawling. No informants threatened with blue hell if they didn't talk. Instead . . . the real thing. Quietly and with little immediate movement. (Jessell and Holmes had been warned to keep their mouths shut. Harper, too; he'd been given the hard word by Sammy Stone.) Eventually, the pace would quicken. When the body had been removed, when the search had been made, when the house-to-house enquiries were under way. *Then* 'pointers' might be encountered. *Then* possible motives might be unearthed. *Then* a direction — possibly more than one direction — might become apparent.

Meanwhile the sensible way — the professional way — was to make haste slowly. Whoever they were after was already three days ahead. Sheer speed was a non-starter. Only methodical plodding — plus, perhaps, a little cunning — would make up the leeway.

THREE

The killers had breakfast at Bordfield Railway Hotel. They had to be sure, and they had to have proof. There was no guarantee that the killing would be reported in the nationals, but it would most certainly earn a front page spread in the local newspaper . . . and they had to *know*.

One of the men refolded the early edition.

He said, 'Nothing.'

'Soon . . . surely.' His companion allowed annoyance to flicker across his expression for a moment.

'Patience.' The first man allowed a sad smile to touch his lips. 'Our greatest strength, my friend. Patience.'

The older man dropped the folded newspaper onto the carpet, alongside his feet, then joined his colleague in eating the breakfast of scrambled egg and toast.

FOUR

By 10 a.m. things were moving. Crowd-control barriers had been brought from Bordfield and the cul-de-sac was sealed off. Phlegmatic coppers had been drafted in from other parts of the division and, under the supervision of Police Sergeant Cockburn from Sopworth, kept the local rubberneckers moving. 'And when the newshounds arrive . . . nowt! Send 'em to me.' The various 'specialist services' were arriving. Photographic Section. Fingerprint Section. Serious Crime Section. Plan Drawing Section. Forensic Liaison Section. Even a shooting brake from the Dog Section. A few of the old lags from the Uniformed Branch sneered open derision. 'Hell's teeth! Why doesn't somebody call out the sub-aqua mob and the Jockey Club. That's all we need . . . a few rubber suits and some nags.'

Blayde and Tallboy stood at the gate of the house and talked in low voices.

'According to Harper, the milk-roundsman, we're three days late.'

'We always *are* late.' Blayde twisted his lips into a lop-sided grin. 'Don't worry, Chris. Do what they all do. Wear the uniform and be happy.'

'Sod the uniform . . . this is *my* midden.'

Blayde cocked an eyebrow. Blayde — Detective Chief Superintendent Robert Blayde — was a cynic. Other than a stray cat which had adopted him, he lived alone in a converted country cottage all of twenty miles from his office at Bordfield Regional Headquarters. It was how he liked things. *His* way. Even when he'd held the same position as Tallboy — chief superintendent in charge of Beechwood Brook Division — he'd lived in that same cottage. The mutterings of disapproval from on high had had no effect. He was the epitome of the word 'loner'. Nor did he kid himself or go in for false modesty. He was a cracker of a detective, he deserved to be Head of Bordfield Region C.I.D. . . . and he knew it.

He also knew the mannerisms of most uniformed superintendents and chief superintendents. Major crime was strictly Plain Clothes Branch business. The guy with the visible pips and crowns had enough on his plate; let the 'Sherlocks' lose sleep over major crime, that being what they were paid for. Way back, Ripley had set a pattern in direct contrast to this widely held theory; if it was 'Beechwood Brook' Ripley had wanted to know. He (Blayde) had followed Ripley's ways; not because he'd been particularly fond of Ripley, but because it had seemed the logical way to run a division with any hope of success. After Blayde, Blakey had screwed things up a little; with Blakey only the rank had mattered, the minor matter of policing a socking great division had been of secondary importance. And now, Tallboy. Ripley's son-in-law, and picking up the thread started by Ripley, continued by Blayde and broken by Blakey.

'All those lost dogs?' teased Blayde sardonically. 'All those bikes without lights?'

Tallboy's nostrils flared and he snapped, 'If you seriously think . . .' He stopped as he saw the twinkle in Blayde's eye, grinned, then said, 'I've a damn good chief inspector. He can earn his corn.'

'Glad of your help, Chris.' Blayde was suddenly very serious. 'As you say . . . we're three days late. We'll need all the bright ideas available.'

Thus the rapport was established. It wasn't difficult. In the past they'd worked together, usually as Blayde the boss and Tallboy a rung or two down the ladder, but throughout there'd been mutual respect. At the back of his mind Blayde knew that Tallboy might eventually step into *his* shoes — God knows, he was good enough — but by that time he (Blayde) would have either retired or upped himself to the post of Assistant Chief Constable (Crime) . . . or some such stratospheric rank.

Meanwhile they waited.

Each murder enquiry varies. There is no set pattern, there never can be. The primary object is not to disturb or destroy clues or pointers. But at the same time a full and extensive record must be compiled of the scene and the area around and leading up to the scene. After that, the search. A slow, methodical sifting of soil and even trash; a ground search, foot at a time — sometimes even inch at a time — inwards, towards the body. And yet not *too* close. To have size tens stamping and thumping within (say) a couple of yards of the body would be asking for trouble; when threads, hairs and even dust can convey information to a trained forensic scientist, it is unwise to allow pavement pounders beyond a certain point.

Thus, in this case, Blayde and Tallboy agreed that the Forensic Liaison Section should ease their way into the house, via the door used by Short and gradually make their way towards the dead woman. That the Serious Crime Section should follow; in effect, acting as long-stop, in case the forensic boys should miss something. The Forensic Liaison and Serious Crime 'specialists' were warned to touch as little as possible and in their wake moved the Fingerprint and Photographic Sections. Thus within the house . . . with the warning that *nobody* must yet touch or disturb the corpse.

Outside the house Police Sergeant Cockburn supervised a search of the surrounding garden. A dozen uniformed constables dirtied their uniform trousers as they (literally) crawled slowly through the tangles of grass and undergrowth and sealed *everything* they found in plastic envelopes, complete with a note of the exact position of its finding. 'And keep in a line. Eyes open for footprints . . . and find 'em, don't *make* 'em. *And* piles of crap. It might be dog-dirt. It might not. If His Nibs was taken short, we want to know what he had for his last meal.' A thankless job for a Sunday morning in October; one of the aspects of a murder hunt *not* emphasised at Police Training Colleges.

Meanwhile Detective Sergeant Kelly and three detective constables were pumping the other residents of the cul-de-sac of as much information as possible.

'Mrs Miller?'

'We'd like to know what you know about her, ma'am.'

'I know one shouldn't speak ill of the dead, but . . .'

'She'll not know.'

'No. Obviously. Well, she was a funny woman.'

'Funny?'

'Strange.'

'In what way?'

'She wouldn't join the local W.I.'

'Shy, possibly?'

'Secretive. I'd call her secretive, rather than shy.'

'Why? What makes you say she was secretive?'

'The way she behaved.'

'Specifically?'

'Well, she kept herself *very* much to herself.'

It was like extracting teeth. Rimstone was a village; a tight little community, with a tight little mentality. You went along with the village activities or you were 'funny', 'odd', 'secretive'. It didn't make the gathering of information any easier. The residents of the cul-de-sac were shocked . . . of course they were. But their shock was related to the crime, not the victim. With more than one of the women it was, very obviously, a personal thing; that they, too, might be attacked and done to death. They weren't too interested — they weren't even too concerned — about the actual *death* of Anne Miller.

Meanwhile, Pinter had arrived at the scene. P.C. 1404 Pinter who shared the beat with Sammy Stone. Wilf Pinter was just about recovering from the shock of losing his wife from terminal cancer . . . and it showed. Humour had not yet returned to his life. His eyes still lived in darkened sockets. There was still a 'zombie' quality to the way he performed his duties. Nevertheless he'd been — and still was — a first class village copper, and his local knowledge, of necessity, exceeded that of Stone.

'Tell us about her,' invited Tallboy.

'She lived alone. I've seen her . . . maybe half a dozen times.

Spoken to her twice.' Pinter paused, pondered for a moment, then continued, 'I think she was unmarried. She didn't wear a wedding ring . . . you'll be able to check on that. She disliked kids. Both times it was a complaint of children playing around the garden. She wasn't popular . . . with her neighbours, I mean.' There was a second pause, then he added, 'I don't think she liked authority.'

'Authority?' Blayde asked the question.

'Policemen, sir. It was just a feeling. She didn't say anything. Just that — y'know — she wasn't keen on bobbies.'

'She should have bought a placard and joined the others,' said Blayde sourly.

'Odd, though,' mused Tallboy. 'She's in the wrong age group.'

'Wrong tense,' grunted Blayde.

'*Was* in the wrong age group.' Tallboy corrected himself. 'They pass middle-age and, unless they're bent, they rather like to be on friendly terms with the local law. It makes 'em feel safer.'

'I got the impression . . .' Pinter stopped.

'Go on,' encouraged Blayde.

'A little unbalanced. Mentally unstable.'

'Potty,' said Blayde bluntly.

'No, sir. Not quite that bad.'

'Who was her doctor?' asked Tallboy.

'I dunno.' Pinter frowned. 'None of the locals. That for sure. I like to know. Then if we need a medic in a hurry I know who to contact.'

'Sniff around,' suggested Blayde. 'They know you . . . they might tell *you* things.'

'There's — er — ' Pinter hesitated, then said, 'There's that Motor Manslaughter file, sir.'

'Pass it to Motor Patrol,' said Tallboy.

'They — er — they won't like . . .'

'The hell with what *they* like,' interrupted Blayde. 'Tell 'em — from me — you're in plain clothes till further notice. You haven't time for road traffic offences.'

Pinter sighed and said, 'Yes, sir.' He looked unhappy. He was that sort of man; he liked finishing whatever he started.

Meanwhile the Forensic Science Liaison Section and the Serious

Crime Section had moved inwards from the porch and almost through the kitchen. The uneaten food had been collected and packed away for examination; its possible condition might give some vague clue as to the last time anybody ate in the house; the pattern of teeth marks on the pieces of bread might prove to be that sliver of extra evidence needed for a future conviction. All 'mights'. All 'maybes'. But crime detection was now a specialised science. Therefore surfaces were squinted at from all angles, the ashes of the dead fire were carefully lifted and packed into a cellophane sack for future scrutiny. Even the dead flowers – even the stinking water in which they'd been standing – was preserved for laboratory examination.

The Photography and Fingerprint Sections formed the second wave of 'searchers'. Like a carefully organised assault upon an enemy beach, they moved in behind Forensic Science Liaison and Serious Crime. The offence was Murder. The Big Fellah. Expense didn't mean a thing. Time didn't matter for the moment. Scores of photographs were taken; three shots from every conceivable angle and distance; three shots of *everything* in case one, or even two, turned out to be duds. White powder and black powder was dusted onto every surface; dusted on with a gentleness which wouldn't have destroyed a cobweb, then flicked off with soft-bristled brushes. What remained was examined; again from every angle and sometimes with the aid of a magnifying glass. Any hint of a fingerprint was 'lifted' carefully on an appropriate length and breadth of Sellotape; an operation which called for a rock-steady hand but which, once completed, 'held' the print for future examination and comparison.

These 'specialists' were aware of the contempt in which they were held by the average working flatfoot. They didn't give a damn; they too – when they'd worn uniform and before they'd learned more sense – had mouthed derisive scorn of the then 'specialists'. 'The Test-tube Babies'. 'The Three-ring Circus'. 'The Brains Trust'. A score of different nicknames, none of them complimentary. But they *knew*. They could smile to themselves with the certainty that time and time again a hair, a handful of debris, a few dozen dust motes and, via microscopes and scientific examination, a villain had been pinned to his villainy.

Meanwhile, the local house-to-house enquiries continued. And this, too, demanded a patience almost beyond the call of duty.

'It's not that I *hated* the woman.'

'No, ma'am, but . . .'

'I wouldn't hate *anybody*.'

'Of course not. But . . .'

'I'm too much of a Christian to *hate* anybody.'

'Quite. But . . .'

'Hatred is something I can never understand.'

'It's — er — it's a bit difficult . . .'

'I mean, why *hate*? It's such a waste of emotion.'

'It is indeed, ma'am. But . . .'

'I believe in love.'

'Good. In that case . . .'

'The power of love, officer. Have you ever considered, officer, how much happier we'd be if love ruled the world?'

'Yes, ma'am. But about . . .'

'Mind you I didn't *like* her.'

'Oh!'

'I didn't *hate* her . . . but I didn't *like* her.'

'Well, we can't all . . .'

'I'll send a wreath, of course.'

'Eh?'

'We owe her that . . . as fellow-Christians.'

'Yes. Of course. But . . .'

'She *was* a Christian, wasn't she?'

'I — er — I dunno. I haven't . . .'

'One never knows, these days, does one?'

'I'm sorry, ma'am, but . . .'

'She certainly didn't *behave* like a Christian, now I come think about it.'

'That's — er — that's none of my . . .'

'Quite obnoxious, in fact.'

'What?'

'Wouldn't even pass the time of day.'

'You mean you . . .'

'Just passing. I'd say 'Good morning' — something like that — and

27

she wouldn't even answer. She'd deliberately ignore me. That's not very *nice*, is it?'

'No. But that's what . . .'

'Rude, in fact.'

'You mean you've talked to her?'

'Talked to her? No. What gives you that impression?'

'You've — you've just said . . .'

'That ignorant old witch. I wouldn't have talked to *her* if we'd been the last two people alive.'

It can be argued that detective constables are working their weary way towards canonisation. That beneath the folds of their unbelted macs the first sprouting of wings might be found. That their periodic headaches are caused by the gradual formation of the halo. That or they live within a self-constructed shell of armour-plating.

Certain it is that a ton of verbal dross must be sifted in order to find one tiny seed pearl of information. It is a heart-breaking occupation. It drives strong men weak, and weak men mad. It ruins marriages, makes for child-beating and brings on alcoholism.

Other than that, it's not a bad job.

'Anything, yet?' asked Detective Sergeant Kelly.

One of his underlings sighed and said, 'For all the good *my* questioning's been, she could have lived on the far side of the moon.'

Kelly said, 'She seems to have been a very private person.'

'Private!'

'Satisfied with her own company.'

'Sarge, she didn't *live* in this bloody world.'

Which (had the outraged detective constable but known it) was no less than the truth.

FIVE

Harris arrived at Sopworth Police Station at a few minutes to noon. The building almost quivered as he strode into the Charge Office. Police Constable 1871 John Henry Higginbottom paled, visibly.

Inspector Rowe moistened his lips, reminded himself that *he* was i/c Sopworth Section, with the blessing of Chief Superintendent Tallboy, and that Chris Tallboy was a divisional officer ready and willing to back his men all the way through hell and out the other side if necessary.

Nevertheless Assistant Chief Constable (Crime) Robert Harris wasn't the sort of guy to be flapped away like some annoying gnat. He was big . . . but *big*. Big in rank, big in stature and big in importance. Maybe not quite as big as he figured himself to be, but big enough to be a mite overpowering if given half the chance.

'What the hell are you doing here?'

Harris's voice was deep and rumbling. In a vocal symphony orchestra he was a dead ringer for the timpani section. He addressed the question to Higginbottom, and Higginbottom swallowed before he answered.

'Office Reserve, sir. Telephone and communications duty.'

'A policewoman could do that.'

'She's — er —'

'She's on holiday, sir.' Rowe stepped in and took the pressure off the unhappy Higginbottom. 'On her honeymoon, actually.'

'Oh?' It was a question, and the question carried the firmly held belief that honeymoons and coppers (male *or* female) didn't mix. He rumbled, 'The Rimstone thing. Any progress yet?'

'They haven't moved the body.'

'Been up there, have you?'

'No, sir. But Chief Superintendent Tallboy hasn't yet rung in for an ambulance.'

'Who's up there? Apart from Tallboy?'

'Mr Blayde. Sergeant Cockburn. Sergeant Kelly. Stone . . . it's his beat, of course. And I've sent Hinton up to lend a hand.'

'That all?'

'I think others have been drafted in, sir. Constables and detectives. I don't know how many.'

'I would hope so,' said Harris drily. 'Otherwise it's all sheriffs and no cowboys.'

'I'm sure they'll have brought other men in, sir.'

'Why do these bloody things always happen on a Sunday?'

complained Harris. It was a daft question, and Rowe didn't feel like giving a daft answer. Harris continued, 'A hanging job, I'm told.'

'Yes, sir. An elderly lady who lived alone.'

'Suicide, happen?'

'I wouldn't think so, sir.' Rowe chose his words with care. 'I doubt whether either Mr Tallboy or Mr Blayde would still be there if it was suicide.'

'A point.' Harris sniffed, then allowed his lips the freedom of a quick half-smile. 'You get on well with Tallboy?'

'He's a fine divisional officer, sir. None better.'

'And,' growled Harris, 'you're not just *saying* that.'

'No, sir. He can show us all the way.'

Harris said, 'I'd better get up there . . . see if he can show *me* the way.'

Sammy Stone had nipped into the kitchen of his home for a quick snack. He'd had damn-all to eat — damn-all to drink — so far that day, and his frame needed steady fuel. He was enjoying the pint mug of scalding hot tea and the fried-egg sandwich. One thing about Elsie, his wife, she could feed a man properly. None of your noodles-this or your rice-the-other. Good grub. Plain grub. Yorkshire grub; very tasty and very filling. This tea, for example. Bugger tea bags; spoon the stuff in and don't be mean. Then Carnation milk and bags of sugar. Strong . . . it damn near dissolved the spoon. A real 'sergeant major' brew. The way tea *should* be made. Same with this sandwich. A plain teacake, sliced into two halves, buttered, then slapped, top and bottom, on a fresh fried egg. A bit messy, maybe; you had to keep an eye on the yolk and lick it off before it spilled all down your front. But there was a knack and a neatly fried, nicely parcelled egg, fresh from the local farm, filled an odd corner or two pending a real meal.

Elsie Stone — a woman as huge as the man she worshipped — entered the kitchen and said, 'All right, is it?'

'Smashing.' Stone sent a fine spray of egg-soaked crumbs as he spoke. He remembered his manners, swigged tea, swallowed, then repeated, 'Smashing.'

'Time will you be in?' asked his wife.

'Dunno. You'd better keep summat warm in the oven, waiting.'

'Meat 'n tater pie?' suggested Mrs Stone.

'Lovely.' Stone nodded. 'It'll keep warm all day if needs be. And red cabbage?'

'It'll be waiting,' promised Mrs Stone. She looked sad, and continued, 'Terrible about Annie Miller, innit?'

'Aye.' Stone nodded.

'Wasn't a bad sort.'

'Why?' Stone looked surprised. 'Did you know her?'

'Not much. I met her once, in the supermarket at Sopworth. We got talking.'

'Oh, aye?'

'Just this and that . . . y'know.'

Sammy Stone 'knew' all right. He loved his wife dearly, weaknesses and all. But he wasn't blind to those weaknesses. He knew, better than anybody, that once Elsie Stone started talking it was like a runaway tank. Nothing would stop her. Nothing *could* stop her. Non-response didn't mean a thing. She still talked. She still asked questions. She battered away until resistance crumbled, and the listener *had* to say something in return. Sometimes, when he was alone on night patrol, Sammy Stone wondered whether those walls of Jericho had fallen for a similar reason; that, among those who trudged around the outside, there'd been somebody with Elsie's monumental gift of the gab.

'What you talk about?' he asked.

'This 'n that,' repeated his wife.

'Yes, but *what*?'

'Weather . . . I think.'

'What else?'

'Price o' things. Nowt spectacular.'

'Look, old luv.' Sammy Stone cleared his mouth; a sort of masticatory de-coking, prior to convincing his wife that what he was about to say was important. 'Mrs Miller. Nobody seems to know a damn thing about her. She musta lived like a bloody hermit. Now, you're the only one who seems to have had a bit of a natter with her. Happen summat. Happen nowt. But try to *remember*. She might have dropped a hint.'

'About what?' Stone's wife looked puzzled.

'Who she was.'

'She was Annie Miller, who else?'

'No. Not that. I mean where she came from. Who her folks were. Why she . . .'

'She was a lonely old woman. That's all. An old Jewish lass who hadn't . . .'

'An old what?'

'Jewish. She was a Jewess.'

'Did she tell you that?'

'What?'

'That she was Jewish?'

'Samuel Stone.' The woman pulled herself into an upright and mildly outraged posture. 'I'm not daft, y'know. I know I married *you*, but that doesn't mean I'm . . .'

'Miller isn't a Jewish name,' said Stone gently.

'I know. Neither's Stone.'

'Stone? You're not suggesting . . .'

'Not *you*, you great fool. Lew Stone. Come to that, Max Miller. There's nowt wrong wi' Jews. Just that Annie Miller was one.'

'Did she tell you?'

'Now, I ask you? *Do* they? Does *anybody*? Do I go about bawling 'Look – I'm a Yorkshire lass.' But everybody knows the minute I open my mouth.'

'Y'mean the way she talked?'

'Aye.' Elsie Stone nodded.

'How?' pressed Stone.

'Y'*know*. The way she talked. The way she turned her sentences back to front a bit. Like when she said the letter 'w'. She couldn't quite get her tongue round it. You can *tell*. She was a Jewess.'

Tallboy and Blayde stared at the corpse. The kitchen and hall had been dealt with, and the Forensic Liaison and Serious Crime crowd had moved into the main living room. All the necessary photographs had been taken, pending further discoveries, and the fine dust from the seekers after fingerprints was starting to settle. An occasional fly settled on the congealed blood at the throat, then spiralled away whenever either of the two men made a sudden movement.

'My God!' breathed Tallboy.

'Assuming there is one,' added Blayde grimly. 'If there is, this is something else He has to answer for.'

They were case-hardened coppers. Both of them. They'd seen corpses before; corpses and bits and pieces of corpses, when some killer had sought to hide his identity by carving up his end-product. But (to both of them) there was something particularly foul about this body of an old lady who — or so it seemed — had lived alone with her minor eccentricity of self-imposed solitude and — again on the face of it — had done nobody any harm. The bulging eyes stared sightlessly from sockets webbed with the creases of age. The open mouth showed teeth, brown and decaying. The neck — scraggy and stretched by the mode of her death — forced the stiffened tendons until they seemed about to burst their way through the surface of the skin. And there was the smell. The sweet and sickly stench of death. Of decaying flesh. Of excreta and urine where the woman had lost final control of her bowels and bladder.

The sight and smell of the aftermath of violence. A bitter thought flicked through Tallboy's mind. That all the penal reform lunatics should be made to look and smell *this*; that they should be made to feel the atmosphere in *this* house. But . . . they wouldn't alter their opinions. Vengeance was not theirs. Understanding. That's what they sought. Understanding, followed by rehabilitation.

But some things were beyond understanding. And some men were beyond rehabilitation. And the only thing left was vengeance. Call it any other name you fancied . . . that's what it *was*. Communal vengeance, meted out to the rogues of the species; the mentally mutated who had no place within a civilised community, and therefore had to be removed for the general good of that community.

'Not robbery,' grunted Blayde.

'What?' Tallboy jerked himself out of his dark imaginings.

'Unless she was one of these oddball types who keep banknotes sewn away in the mattress.'

'Oh! — er — not robbery. Not if what we've seen has anything to . . .' Tallboy stopped, ran fingers through his greying hair, then whispered, 'Who the hell deserves *this*? This sort of death?'

'No gag,' observed Blayde flatly.

Blayde — maybe because he *was* Blayde — showed no hint of emotion. Stone-faced. His voice devoid of all expression. Looked at from the viewpoint of normal humanity, Blayde was a little frightening. He was as near to a machine as no-matter . . . or so it seemed. As at this moment, he was capable of viewing vileness without blinking an eyelid. It didn't upset him. Equally, he didn't glorify in it. Dispassionately, quietly, coolly, he evaluated the externals of evil and, having weighed the pros and cons, he reached a decision.

He grunted, 'Ritual. That's the first impression.'

'Who the hell would want to . . .'

'When we find him, we'll ask. Then if he tells us, we'll know.'

'Him?' Tallboy forced himself to concentrate.

'*Them*.' Blayde corrected himself. 'She was overpowered. She was tied up. She was lifted, and strung up there. I'd say more than one.'

'She — she may have been knocked out,' contributed Tallboy.

'Possibly. But lifting a dead-weight — even her — and hooking it over those pegs. Not easy for one man. I'd say more than one.'

'More than one,' agreed Tallboy.

'No gag, though. Assuming she wasn't knocked out . . . she'd scream.'

'*I'd* scream,' admitted Tallboy.

'Somebody should have heard her. Out here, little traffic. Never noisy . . . not like in a town. Somebody should have heard her.'

'Maybe they did,' suggested Tallboy heavily. 'If so, we'll get to 'em, eventually.'

'Chris.' Blayde turned his attention from the body. His tone had a friendly, but paternal, quality. 'Knock it off, Chris. It's getting to you . . . it shouldn't. It's just another corpse. Dead meat. Something from a butcher's slab. And that's *all* it is. Make it any more, and you'll be more of a hindrance than a help.'

Tallboy nodded sadly.

'I want your help,' added Blayde. 'As a copper . . . not as a mourner.'

Rimstone village had never seen the like before. Each summer it organised its own little fête and, within the strict limits of its meagre budget, it put on quite a show; people had been known to travel all of ten miles to take part in the festivities. The lads from the local Young Farmers branch put on a New Year's Ball, and this, too, was not to be sneezed at; the village hall was festooned with holly, bunting and balloons, a four-piece band — piano, drums, fiddle and guitar — sweated buckets as they churned out every number in their restricted repertoire over and over again, and feet more accustomed to wellies defied corns and bunions in an effort to go one better than the Savoy Ballroom.

All this, plus the W.I., plus the church outing . . . but nothing like *this*.

In life, Annie Miller had been brushed aside as a silly old woman with peculiar ways. In death she'd put Rimstone on the map. Television cameras, no less. And radio interviewers. To say nothing of ladies and genetlemen, with their attendant photographers, from both local and national newspapers. They talked to just about anybody prepared to talk back. 'You knew Mrs Miller?' 'Naw.' 'You live here in Rimstone?' 'Oh, aye.' 'You mean she wasn't very neighbourly?' 'Dunno. *I'm* not very neighbourly.' 'You know she's dead, of course?' 'Oh, aye. It cooms to us all, lad. Bide thi time, lad . . . tha'll be dead i' time.' The vicar was more obliging. He even brushed his hair in order that he might look a little less mad than usual. 'A good woman. I'm sure she was.' 'You knew her?' '*Of* her. She wasn't part of my congregation.' 'Not Church of England?' 'One presumes not. She never attended church.'

Harris started as he meant to go on. A cub reporter, anxious to earn himself a by-line on one of the nationals barred his path as he unfolded himself from his Rover and prepared himself for the launching of necessary rockets.

'Detective Chief Superintendent Harris . . . am I right?'

'Up a bit, lad.'

'I — er — I beg your pardon?'

'Assistant Chief Constable Harris.'

'Oh! You're in charge here, sir, am I right?'

'Unless you have a spare chief constable tucked up your sleeve.'

'Quite. Now, sir, what information can you give me?'

'Very personal, lad.'

'Ah!'

'If you don't shift yourself — *now* — you'll find yourself booked for Police Obstruction.'

In the evening edition, the cub reporter got his own back. The paragraph read 'Detective Chief Superintendent *Haggis* stated that he had personal information he was not prepared to divulge.'

Meanwhile A.C.C. (Crime) Harris advanced like a one-man Panzer division. His job — as he saw it — was to ginger things up a little. This, translated into ordinary language, meant that he sought and found fault with every copper he passed. 'When the hell did you last have a haircut, lad? Much longer and you'll have people treading on the bloody stuff as they pass.' 'Which mob do *you* think you belong to, constable? The Paratroop Regiment? That's a helmet you're wearing, lad, not a beret. Get it on straight.' And, to one ancient and utterly fireproof member of the British Police Service, 'What the devil are you doing *here*, officer? You should be back there, keeping the crowds back.' 'Ballocks.' '*What*?' '*Bullocks*, sir. I'm told some might be driven this way, soon. We don't want 'em tramping all over the nice new clues . . . do we?'

Eventually he reached Blayde and Tallboy; joined them in eyeing the corpse.

'Ideas?' he grunted.

'Not many,' admitted Blayde expressionlessly.

'What's missing?'

'She can't tell us,' said Blayde with gentle sarcasm.

'Nothing obvious.' Tallboy jumped in to prevent what would undoubtedly have developed into a heavyweight slanging championship. 'From what we've been able to see not much . . . if anything.'

'What about 'The Brains'?' Harris jerked his head, with all the overpowering contempt of a man who'd bulldozed his way to the top.

'They're checking the living room,' said Tallboy. 'Then they'll start upstairs.'

'What about moving her? She's starting to pong a bit.'

Blayde said, 'I want Carr to have a decko before we lift her down.'

Harris sniffed reluctant approval, growled, 'Right. Keep on top.

Keep me informed,' turned and strode back towards his parked Rover.

'And,' murmured Blayde, 'with those words of ancient wisdom the Great White Chief walked proudly into the sunset.'

There being, you see, no such thing as complete objectivity within the Police Service. The 'Starsky and Hutch' image notwithstanding, unqualified friendship, unqualified trust is *not* part of the complete copper's makeup. Nor should it be. The very essence of his trade — particularly if he works in C.I.D. — is based upon suspicion. He suspects everybody and everything. At times, he even suspects the evidence of his own senses. That, for starters. Of necessity, he upturns the basic tenet of British Justice. Everybody is guilty until proved innocent. And, moreover, that proof has to be conclusive.

A buddy-buddy relationship between two coppers, therefore, is a rare — almost an unknown — thing. There may be trust, there may be respect, there may be mutual admiration . . . but there is rarely deep-down friendship. The nearest thing to genuine friendship is that which existed between Blayde and Tallboy; a liking, backed by a knowledge that the other guy knew his job backwards.

Away from the centre of high activity Constables Stone and Pinter were exchanging opinions. They'd met each other by chance, and Stone sought advice from his colleague, who'd bobbied the beat for some number of years.

'The missus says 'Jewish',' explained Stone.

'Maybe.' Pinter's sad eyes took on an expression of thought.

'She's talked to her,' explained Stone. 'The old lass can clack a bit . . . and she says Annie Miller was a Jewess. The way she talked.'

'Possible,' agreed Pinter.

'You've talked to her a few times.'

'A couple of times,' agreed Pinter.

'What d'you think?'

'She didn't speak good English,' agreed Pinter. 'Maybe a foreign accent.'

'A *Jewish* accent?' pressed Stone.

Pinter nodded.

'Y'see,' explained Stone, 'if she was it may be important. But if she *wasn't*, I'm gonna look a bit of a nerk.'

'Some people lisp.' Pinter wasn't being too helpful. 'Other people . . .' He moved his shoulders.

'Jesus Christ, I wish I was sure,' muttered Stone.

'Tell 'em,' advised Pinter. 'Maybe she *was* a Jewess.'

'Kelly, you think?' suggested Stone.

'Kelly?'

'Tell Kelly. See what he says?'

'Tell Tallboy,' said Pinter wearily. 'If you tell Kelly, *he'll* tell Tallboy. And Blayde. Then, they'll want to see you . . . and want to know why *you* didn't tell 'em in the first place.'

'Oh hell,' breathed Stone.

'Sammy.' Pinter gave a quick, sad smile. 'Do it the easy way. Just tell 'em.'

Dr Joseph Carr, M.Sc., Ph.D., director of the Area Forensic Science Laboratory. Such an ordinary-everybody-looking chap. Not very tall, a mite on the stout side, going thin on top. Dark suit, white shirt with a dark tie, black shoes . . . but no dandy. Even his bosom friends wouldn't have called him a dandy, nor even neatly dressed. *Ever*.

Some men have this ability. Take the finest tailor in the land, the finest shirt-maker, the finest hairdresser, the finest shoe-maker. It would all be a waste of time and money. The end-product would *still* be a walking rag-bag. But with Carr, the sort of personality capable of making clothes and appearance utterly superfluous. He looked the perfect 'favourite uncle' type . . . indeed, he *was* a favourite uncle to umpteen nieces and nephews.

And yet he dealt in horror; real-life horror, not the make-believe stuff of which motion pictures are made. His bodies were dead and, in the main, violated. His exhumations stank to the high heaven of rotting flesh and maggots. His day-to-day trade would have made most undertakers shudder and puke their hearts out.

He stood close to the hanging corpse, raised a hand, plucked a tiny portion of the congealed blood from around the wire, then rubbed the blood between forefinger and thumb.

'She was alive,' he said sombrely.

He turned the body, felt at the tips of the dead fingers, then bent and examined the nails.

'Three days?' he murmured.

'About that,' agreed Blayde.

'It fits. She was a moderately heavy smoker.'

'How old?' asked Tallboy.

Carr sucked in his breath, re-examined the fingers, turned the corpse, lifted the upper lip to check the teeth, touched the stretched neck muscles.

'Sixty . . . a round figure,' he pronounced.

'I'd have thought older,' said Blayde.

'Give or take five years,' said Carr. 'We may get closer with the post mortem.' He glanced round and asked, 'No Birth Certificate?'

'Nothing,' said Blayde flatly. 'No books, no papers. Not even newspapers. As far as documents are concerned, she didn't exist.'

'You've searched, of course?'

'*I've* searched,' said Blayde, and the implication was that the search had been complete and couldn't be bettered.

Tallboy said, 'Nobody does that accidentally, doc.'

'What?'

'Leave *nothing*. There's always . . . something. If it's only a hint. Letters. Old addresses, phone numbers . . . something.'

'She must have been registered with a doctor . . . surely?'

'Nothing,' repeated Blayde.

'Mmm.' Carr returned his attention to the body. He gazed up at the head, and above the head at the peg from which she hung.

'Piano wire,' he said gently.

'I'd have made a guess,' said Blayde. 'I've suggested ritual.'

'Of a sort,' agreed Carr. He turned. His face was unaccustomedly troubled. When he spoke it was in a low, worried tone. 'The Nazis used it. The concentration camps. Hitler wanted a record. Something he could see. Something he could show his friends. They hung 'em on meat-hooks. Used piano wire. Took moving pictures of 'em dying. The — er — the film's still around somewhere.'

Carr stopped talking. He kept his head bowed, as if in token respect for victims of a madman's outrage. Blayde and Tallboy remained silent. For a few seconds – just for a few seconds – the terrible hopelessness of a once-upon-a-time death scene, in a stinking windowless room of a faraway concentration camp touched the hallway of an ugly house in a northern village.

Blayde's voice was almost unrecognisable, as he rasped, 'This one's going to be detected, Chris. If I have to work every man in this force until he drops . . . *this one's going to be detected.*'

Tallboy breathed, 'Amen to that.'

There was a sound from the rear. They turned and watched Stone as he walked through the kitchen.

Stone cleared his throat, then said, 'Sir . . .' He spoke directly to Tallboy, because Tallboy was his immediate boss. 'Sir, I've come across something I think you should know. Something – y'know – it might help. I – er – I think she was a Jewess.'

It could have been called a 'Council of War'. Or, in less emotive language, it could have been called an exchange of ideas – a co-ordination of known facts, plus an airing of opinions – but whatever term might be used, it amounted to the same thing. Rowe's office at Sopworth Police station was the venue and, although it wasn't a particularly small office, it was crowded. Blayde and Tallboy were there, so were Kelly and Cockburn. Rowe was there, too, if only because it was his office. Stone and Pinter were there; the crime had been committed on their beat. Kyle was there; Kyle's beat was Upper Neck, but he was the sort of copper likely to know many things about his neighbouring beat also. Carr was there and, with him, the pathologist who'd performed the post mortem examination on the murdered woman. And the whole get-together was presided over by Harris.

It was closing up to 10 p.m. In the Charge Office, Sergeant Berry was handing the section over to Sergeant Ramsden. Constables Wooley and Barker had already arrived, and P.C. Sowe (who'd been holding a one-man fort in the absence of his colleague, Hinton, on the house-to-house enquiry) was happy to breathe more easily in the knowledge that Sopworth Town was no longer a 'one man band'.

In Rowe's office the smoke from cigarettes, pipes and a cheroot rose to curl in spirals and clouds around the strip lighting. All the chairs were occupied, but most of the occupants of the office were ranged against the walls.

Harris was holding forth.

'. . . a statement from everybody who lives at Rimstone. I don't care whether they live within hearing distance of the crime or not. Every man, woman and child. Everything they can remember since last Sunday. Any strangers. Any vehicles they didn't recognise. The ordinary and the out-of-the-ordinary. We want to dovetail those statements together and, from 'em, know every damn thing that happened in that village for a whole week.

'From there we move outwards. The statements will tell us who visited the village and when. We want statements from *them*. All of 'em. Friends, relations, delivery people . . . the lot. Somebody saw something. Somebody heard something. And don't anybody tell me they didn't. Somebody. And I want a statement from that 'Somebody'.

'Tomorrow morning — first thing — I want an Incident Centre set up. The village hall, alongside the vicarage. Any arguments, refer them to Chief Superintendent Blayde . . .'

'Or to me,' cut in Tallboy.

'Or to Chief Superintendent Tallboy,' agreed Harris. 'One of 'em won't be far away.' Harris paused then, with a suitable catch in his voice, fed the old hearts-and-flowers routine to men who'd listened to too much schmaltz to be fooled. 'An elderly Jewish lady. Living alone. Minding her own business. Hurting nobody . . .'

Tallboy listened with mild disgust. He knew Harris and, at moments like this, Harris could have collected every Oscar in creation. To Harris a corpse was a corpse, and that's *all* it was. Sure he wanted the murder detected, but for purely *police* reasons. Undetected murder looked bad on the crime stats and, moreover, triggered off pointed questions, come the H.M.I. inspection. The truth was, Annie Miller was an infernal nuisance as far as Harris was concerned. Her manner of death interfered with the smooth running of the Criminal Investigation Department.

Eventually, Harris boxed his violin, put aside the orchids and allowed Carr to say his piece. The chubby scientist didn't waste words. He talked facts; facts which had come from a recently performed post mortem; facts which were based upon a first sort-through of the cellophane bags and envelopes deposited at the laboratory.

'She died on the wire. She was alive when they strung her up there. There was no great struggle. At a guess, she was too weak to struggle. The wire . . . piano wire. Easily get-at-able. But at the same time, not available at the nearest hardware shop. Her hands and feet were tied with nylon cord. Clothes-line stuff. Miles of it sold every day. No fingerprints, other than those of the dead woman. Subject to closer scrutiny, no pointers from what was taken from the house or garden. She smoked. Without actually starving herself, she ate little. No fridge. No freezer. Very little food in the pantry. No documents . . . that's something very unusual. No letters, no photographs, no birthday cards, no cheque book. Nothing. If the postman called — something you'll be able to establish — she must have burned, or destroyed, everything he delivered.'

He paused and, obviously, awaited possible questions.

Rowe cleared his throat and said, 'There's a suggestion she was Jewish.'

'Yes.' Carr nodded. 'From people who've heard her speak. The letter 'w'. She had difficulty in pronouncing it. It sounded more like 'v'. The local vicar says she never went to church. Pointers. But we're pretty sure she was a Jewess.'

Again Carr awaited questions.

Kelly asked, 'Any idea how long she'd lived there?'

Tallboy answered and said, 'A line of enquiry, sergeant. We start it tomorrow. How long? Who lived there before? Which house agent — which solicitor — was used.' He smiled at the D.S. and added, 'Your pigeon, sergeant?'

'Thank you, sir.'

The pathologist came next. He used ten-cylinder words, but merely added to what Carr had already said or hinted at. The body of a woman; height and weight; under-nourished a little, but not particularly unhealthy; age approximately sixty years; no scars, no operation marks; married or not, she wasn't a virgin, but there were no obvious signs of her having given birth to a child; three of her teeth were goldcapped; the heart showed signs of a mild attack some few years ago. Yes, she smoked, but, by the state of the lungs, not heavily. No, there were no marks of bruising . . . whoever had manhandled her to the hall clothes-peg hadn't had to use too much violence.

Blayde had the last word.

He stared at the watching officers and said, 'That's it, then. From here on, it's a steady slog. Priorities. *My* priorities. Find out who the hell she was . . . other than Annie Miller. As much as possible about her. Doesn't matter how trivial. Anything! Don't bung your minds up with fanciful "motives". Let's know *who* she was – *what* she was – then we've a firm base to build on. Questions. That's what it boils down to. Enough questions and we'll come up with enough answers.'

SIX

At the Bordfield Railway Hotel the killers sat at their table and waited for their usual breakfast of scrambled eggs and toast. The elder of the two men unfolded the local newspaper.

The headline read:

JEWISH WOMAN SLAIN IN RITUAL MURDER

The elder man closed his eyes, as if in despair, then passed the newspaper across the table to his companion.

The younger man glanced at the headline, then gasped, 'Oh, my God!'

'Retribution,' murmured the elder man sadly.

At that moment the waiter arrived at the table with their food.

SEVEN

The village was between Wismar and Schwerin, in the Prussian province of Mecklenburg; a tiny village of not much more than a thousand souls, tucked away in a fold of the pine forest and within easy walking distance of the shore of the broad lake. A beautiful village; the most beautiful, the most peaceful, the most perfect village in all Germany. In all the world. Or so thought Walter Schnitzler, the village bookseller, and never was he more certain than on the afternoon of June 3rd, 1923, when his wife, Ninja, presented him with a daughter. A daughter of his own; a friend for little Hannah . . . the two-year-old Hannah, his niece, who'd lived with them since the death of her parents less than a year ago. It was a good life, a good world, with himself the head of his tiny family of females . . . what man could ask for more?

Five years since the end of The War. Germany was gradually becoming great again. Slowly, but as surely as tomorrow's sunrise. Here in Mecklenburg, memories of the old Imperialism glowed and were glorified. Faith in the dethroned Kaiser — their beloved Kaiser — whose defeat was a mere temporary inconvenience. The great landowners were born to rule. Prussian pride was far too great ever to suffer humiliation.

Oh yes, there was the other thing, of course. That lunatic, chauvinistic doctrine of some upstart called Hitler. Silly, of course. All those stupid slogans, those ridiculous flags, those outrageous myths. A flash in the pan; the rantings of a rabble-rouser whose temporary pseudo-ideology was brought from Berlin and the other cities by week-ending motorists. But Prussia — Mecklenburg — never in a thousand years.

Herr Schnitzler smiled at such foolishness. He had a daughter, Helena. He had his niece, Hannah Muller, daughter of his dead sister and, to Herr Schnitzler, a second daughter and an elder sister to his real daughter. He had his beloved wife, Ninja.

He had his books and his bookshop.

Could any man ask for more?

In the Presidential election of 1932 seven out of the thirty-five German constituencies voted for the 'upstart'. Mecklenburg was one of the seven. Herr Schnitzler, although surprised — even disappointed — didn't worry. The old 'man of iron', Hindenburg, would keep the loud-mouthed puppet well under control.

Meanwhile, and this to their credit, the 'Hitler people' could certainly organise both outdoor and indoor activities for young girls. Songs and discussions at various halls in and around the village almost every evening of the week. Camping holidays, with sing-songs round the fire. And the young men who organised these things were to be trusted; good Germans — considerate of parental anxiety — the type of men (and sometimes young women) to whom a father could hand over temporary guardianship of his children without fear. The youth of The Fatherland were a credit to the nation, and Helena and Hannah grew healthier and more vital as they moved towards their teens.

At first, Herr Schnitzler approved; even gave gentle encouragement to the two girls in their eagerness to learn a love of the countryside, a patriotism for the German soil, a near-worship of Wagnerian heroes. It was right that they should know the glory of their country. That they should be true Germans . . . true Prussians.

Ninja would sometimes shake her head and say, 'Walter, I hear rumours. I hear the girls talking together sometimes. I think it would be wise not to allow them quite so much freedom. Expose them to quite so much politics.'

'You worry, Ninja.' Schnitzler would smile his love for his wife. 'They are young. Let them feed. Let them gorge themselves. In time, they will learn to separate the good from the bad. They have a fine home. They will know, without being taught.'

Nevertheless, Frau Schnitzler continued to worry and when, in 1936, Helena came home from her school and announced that she was now a member of the BDM — the Nazi League of German Maidens — Frau Schnitzler showed her worry in open anger.

'Such nonsense. Politics, at your age.'

'Mamma, I am not a child. I am . . .'

'You are still a child, you foolish girl. This Hitler and his stupidity. He should be ashamed! He should . . .'

'You will not talk of our Leader in that way.'

The elder woman paled at the clenched-teeth fury with which her daughter had spat out the words. For a moment, she stood. Then, for the first time in her life, she struck her daughter with the desire to really hurt. No warning tap across the wrist, but a full-blooded, open-handed swing which left a scarlet imprint on the girl's face.

Helena's expression froze as she fought back the tears, then she turned and ran up the stairs to her bedroom.

Frau Schnitzler wept also. She wept for a way of life she had once known; for the gradual, post-war stabilisation which, thanks to this new-fangled National Socialism, seemed to be slipping from the Fatherland's grasp. This Hitler . . . he was a fool. How could he expect children still at school to understand? Anything? What experience of life had they? What basic yardstick, via which they could measure good against evil?

She dried her eyes and sloshed water over her face before the arrival home of Hannah. Hannah had already left school; she'd found work on one of the local farms. Unskilled work, but hard work. To greet her with a tear-stained face wouldn't help. What was more, Walter was the head of the house. The problem was his. He must drag his nose from his stupid books, return to the world of reality, if only long enough to convince Helena of the callowness of her ways. Of the stupidity of becoming enmeshed in this Nazi way of life before she was old enough to reach a personal decision.

Poor Walter Schnitzler. So wise, and yet so child-like. So gentle, and therefore unable to counter the steel which had been carefully forged into his daughter's personality.

The two girls stood in front of him, while Frau Schnitzler sat in a shadowed corner of the room, listening and watching. Listening to the sorrow of the daughter who wasn't her daughter, and the open defiance of the daughter who was.

'You should have asked,' said Schnitzler sadly. 'You should have sought guidance from either your mamma or myself.'

'It was necessary,' said Helena coldly.

'Necessary?'

'It was automatic. The law requires all schoolgirls to join the Nazi League of German Maidens.'

'It does not 'require',' said Walter, mildly. 'It merely says 'you may'.'

'I desired to.'

'Without consultation?'

'The branch leader said I should.'

'The — er — branch leader?'

'The group leader instructed him to tell me.'

'Leaders,' sighed Walter. 'So many leaders . . . yet all follow, like so many sheep.'

'You do not understand.'

'True.' Walter removed his spectacles. He pinched the root of his nose, then nodded. 'All my life I have sought knowledge. I have studied the writings of great men. Great thinkers. Men with great minds. All my life I have tried, but I do *not* understand.'

'You're an old man,' sneered Helena. 'The world is ours. You had your chance and you were hoodwinked.'

'Did your leader tell you that, too?' There was an unaccustomed bite to Walter's words.

'History tells us that,' snapped Helena.

'Your history. A twisted history.' Walter looked into the face of his daughter and said, 'If you were my son I would thrash you. I would knock sense in and stupidity out.'

'You wouldn't dare . . .'

'I am your papa,' snapped Walter. 'I have authority in this house. Your precious 'leader' seems to have besotted you with his perverted ideals . . . but *I* still have final say. The Nazi League of German Maidens! What are you? Some schoolgirl organisation similar to the so-called 'cheer-leaders' I read about in America? Will you be learning ridiculous chants, perhaps? Will you be exhibiting yourself at stadiums?' He turned his head and looked at the elder girl. Then, in a less harsh voice, asked, 'And you, Hannah? Do you also intend to join this silly 'league'?'

Before she could answer Helena said, 'Jewesses are not included in our ranks.'

The stark brutality with which the words were spoken brought a silence. For a few moments the horror of things yet to be touched the room, and Herr Schnitzler and his wife felt the cold wind of a passing emotional maelstrom.

Frau Schnitzler almost choked the words, 'Helena! You will go to your room. *Now*. You will stay there until you are ready to apologise to your papa and to Hannah. You shame this house with your foul talk. You shame this family. Go . . . *now*!'

Helena Schnitzler didn't answer. A slow, sardonic smile touched her lips as she turned and marched, rather than walked, from the room.

Herr Schnitzler replaced his spectacles. The anger had gone from his expression. Sorrow and puzzlement was there in abundance. That, and genuine parental affection, as he looked sadly at the face of the girl he always thought of as an elder daughter. He saw the tears spill from the eyes and roll gently down her cheeks and, for some strange reason, he felt guilt and shame. *His* guilt. *His* shame. But he didn't know why.

'Am I?' The question was less than a whisper.

'What?' Walter Schnitzler pretended not to understand.

'A Jew?' she breathed.

'No. No . . . of course not.' He waved a hand, as if the question was a minor annoyance.

'My — my father?'

'He was a good man. A close friend . . .'

'I mean . . .'

'He married my sister. I was glad for her. She deserved such a man. He was . . .'

'Was he a Jew?'

'Hannah, my child, he would have been a fine father. A better father than I can ever . . .'

'Was he a Jew?' she repeated.

'He was a German. A *good* German. There was nothing . . .'

'Please tell me,' she pleaded.

Walter Schnitzler nodded, slowly. He ran his fingers through the iron grey of his hair.

'It isn't important, Hannah.' The sorrow in his voice passed the pain he felt across the room to his wife. 'That he was a good man — that he was a good *German* — that is all. Be proud to be his daughter. Believe me, he would have been proud to have been your father. Nothing else. The other things are stupidities. Helena didn't mean it. You will see. She will apologise — her and her silly League of German Maidens — she will apologise.'

'No.' Despite the tears, her voice was steady now. 'She will not apologise. That would not be allowed.' She tried hard to smile, almost succeeded, sniffed, then said, 'I will go for a walk. To be alone. To think a little. And . . . thank you for telling me.'

They made no attempt to stop her. They tried to understand. Indeed, they *thought* they understood. But they didn't; they were not of a generation to understand.

The next morning Helena Schnitzler left home and never returned.

EIGHT

The vicar murmured ecclesiastical words of disapproval. The members of the Mother's Union were outraged. The ladies of the W.I. threatened everything up to, and including, 'Questions in the House'. But the coppers didn't give a damn. The village hall, alongside the vicarage, became an Incident Centre; a murder had been committed, therefore Bible classes, knitting circles and jam and Jerusalem were at liberty to take a running jump . . . and good luck to 'em.

Oddly enough, the vicar's wife was delighted. She was a 'thriller' enthusiast; she devoured the things at a steady rate of anything up to half-a-dozen a week. She'd read everything penned by Erle Stanley Gardner (which was no mean feat) and, had she had her way, Chandler would have been deified and given place of honour among the figures picked out in the stained-glass window. Her current heroes were Symons, Macdonald and Wambaugh.

'You will let me come in and out,' she pleaded. 'I won't get in the way . . . I promise. And I won't tell. Not even my husband.'

'You have the wrong idea, ma'am.' Tallboy smiled and glanced around at the trestle-tables, the shoe-boxes to be used as makeshift card-indexes, the two battered typewriters, the Post Office engineers busy installing two telephones and (above all else) the still-cartoned stack of witness forms, typing and carbon paper and foolscap. 'I doubt if you'll find one magnifying glass. And, if a bloodhound strolls in, it'll be reported as a lost dog.'

'You're teasing me,' she accused.

'It *is* boring,' Tallboy assured her.

'But interesting . . . to me, at any rate.'

'All right.' Tallboy sighed, grinned and nodded. He added, 'But be warned. Coppers tend to use juicy language . . . especially when they're tired and getting nowhere.'

'I know.' She returned the grin. 'Some of the books I've read. I know all the words.'

'You'll never make Heaven,' chuckled Tallboy.

'Y'know . . .' She held her head on one side. 'If some of the people I know — who are so sure *they're* going — it's likely to be a very dull place.'

She turned and left and, for a moment, Tallboy hoped the vicar knew how lucky he was. Then he strolled over to a detective sergeant. Detective Sergeant Reese.

Reese was fingering his way through the small accumulation of bumph which was already occupying one of the tables. He was a good D.S., and this for one very simple reason. He was a puzzle fanatic. Give him a puzzle — crossword, jigsaw, cypher, any sort of puzzle — and he was happy. He loved finding answers. His mind was tidy and unhurried; where other people cut string tying a parcel, Reese fiddled and fingered the knots until they were undone. Okay, he wanted to know what was in the parcel but to *get* that knowledge the untying of knots was necessary. D.S. Reese was a grinder, and Tallboy had all the time on earth for grinders . . . in the long term, they brought home a damn sight more bacon than the glory boys.

'Sorry to bring you in from Bordfield,' said Tallboy. 'I hope it hasn't meant leaving too much in the pending tray.'

Reese moved his shoulder resignedly.

Tallboy said, 'Want a quick run-down on the case?'

'I've read the reports.' Reese motioned towards the papers. 'I've also been across to the house.'

'You must have been here with the sparrows.'

'Gold-capped teeth and that dump. They don't go together.'

'It doesn't quite fit,' agreed Tallboy.

'You can't get 'em National Health.' Reese pushed the logic carefully along. 'More than that. You can't get 'em private, except from some of the fancy dentists. Gold caps . . . very pricey. But, having got 'em, she hadn't much to chew *with* 'em.'

'Point taken,' agreed Tallboy.

'No fridge. No deep-freeze. Not enough food in the house to choke a cat.' Reese looked at Tallboy questioningly. 'My line?' he asked.

'Need any help?'

'No, sir.' Reese hesitated. 'A template of the teeth — gold-caps and all — might be useful.'

'Doc Carr,' suggested Tallboy. 'Tell him you've my authority.'

'Thanks.' Reese nodded briefly, then left the Incident Centre.

Tallboy watched him go and pondered upon the possibility that this young man — this Detective Sergeant Reese — might be on the first rung of a very long ladder. He had his own knack of picking a certain line of enquiry, then pushing it quietly to the very end. Okay — if the gold-capped teeth led to a blind alley, so what? — Reese would return to the Incident Centre, poke around until he found two other pieces that didn't quite fit, then move off again from there. A 'style' peculiar to himself. A 'trademark'.

Cars drew up outside the village hall and Kelly and Rowe entered. Kelly made for the papers Reese had been reading. Rowe joined Tallboy.

'Bill,' greeted Tallboy.

'Just a quick look-in, sir.' Rowe smiled. 'Anything you need from Sopworth?'

'Men,' said Tallboy, mischievously. Then, added, 'I know, you'll have to draw 'em on the wall.'

'I could stretch things a little more,' offered Rowe.

'No.' Tallboy shook his head, then opened a packet of cigarettes and held it for Rowe to take one. 'Sergeant Cockburn, P.C. Hinton and the outside men. They'll do for the moment. I'll bring in others from other sections.'

'Just ask.' Rowe flicked a lighter and held the flame to Tallboy's, then his own, cigarette. 'I'll have a word with the traffic lads. Get 'em to drive round the section a few times.'

Tallboy said, 'Post mortem results. I've had 'em duplicated. The inquest's this afternoon. Stone'll be there. I can leave that to you?'

'Sure.' Rowe inhaled cigarette smoke. 'I'll let you know the result.'

'Opened, then adjourned at a guess.'

'At a guess,' agreed Rowe. He asked, 'Anything new since last night's briefing?'

Tallboy shrugged. 'Blayde has this bee in his bonnet. That her name's *not* Annie Miller. Tip the wink to the coroner. Off the record.'

'Will do.'

They smoked in silence for a moment, and Tallboy wondered at the change in this man. Inspector William Henry Rowe. When Blakey had headed Beechwood Brook Division he'd been a perpetually frightened man; a man worried almost to the point of ulcers about not being up to his job. Blakey's fault, of course. Blakey'd been a useless bastard, ever ready to sling blame on everybody else's shoulders. It had damn near spoiled Rowe as a copper. Now — given the responsibility, and the knowledge that the only clangers he'd be expected to carry were his own — Rowe was a changed man. He'd never be a drag-'em-out-and-kick-their-teeth-in type. He wasn't made that way. But very reliable and no longer afraid.

Tallboy noted the change. Noted that the change had coincided with his own promotion to Beechwood Brook Divisional Officer but (had he been asked) that's what he'd have called it. A coincidence. That or the removal of Blakey. Not for a moment would he have connected *his* appointment with Rowe's changed attitude to policing. Like all the nice guys, Tallboy under-estimated himself and, at the same time, under-estimated the effect he had on other people.

They talked and smoked for a few minutes. Detective constables and members of the uniformed branch, in plain clothes, arrived at the Incident Centre. Then Rowe left for Sopworth Police Station, Tallboy squashed what was left of his cigarette into a tobacco tin doing duty as an ash-tray, and set about the first full day's real enquiries.

Pinter drove over from Upper Neck beat and picked up Andy Kyle before they continued on to the Incident Centre. Since the death of

Pinter's wife they'd become more than colleagues working adjoining beats. Both quiet men — Kyle on the dour side, Pinter shy in the company of strangers — they enjoyed each other's company without the need to talk too much. Yet, when the need arose to talk they seemed to have developed a verbal shorthand in which a word became a sentence and a sentence a whole speech.

Pinter drove the mini-van, while Kyle enjoyed his first cigarette of the day. The lanes between the house and the Incident Centre held an overlay of fallen leaves, wet and slippery from the night's dampness. The holly which formed part of the hedgerows was already spotted with red berries, the long grass of the verges was limp and dying and, overhead, the unbroken cloud showed gunmetal grey and gave promise of rain yet to come.

'Stone says a Jewess,' murmured Kyle.

'His wife.' Pinter kept his eyes on the road ahead.

'You've spoken to her.'

'Only twice.'

'And?'

'Not English.'

There was a silence, then Kyle said, 'Jewess means Kosher.'

'Not always.'

'Orthodox.'

'Not many about.'

'Not in the country,' agreed Kyle.

There was more silence then, as he turned into the lane leading to the village hall, Pinter said, 'The flowers puzzle me.'

'Not from the garden,' agreed Kyle.

'A present?' suggested Pinter.

'Flowers before food?' Kyle answered a question with another question.

'There might be a reason.'

Pinter drew the mini-van in behind Kelly's car, then they climbed out and walked towards the Incident Centre.

Blayde was driving in from his isolated cottage at a greater rate of knots. The 1.3 Fiesta held the road beautifully and the open window alongside his right shoulder brought in the sharp tang of cold upland air to dispel the last thickness of a restless night.

The trick (or so preached Blayde) was never to 'take work home'. To do as much as possible, as well as possible then, at the end of the day, to step from one world to another . . . and forget it. Fine advice, but advice he himself hadn't been able to follow.

Damn the woman! Who the hell *was* she? Annie Miller? Annie Miller my foot! Bodies — even murdered bodies — retained an identity and, moreover, left proof of their identity . . . especially if they were done to death in their own home. But this one! Every last blasted pointer had been removed. And not by the killer or killers. By *her*. It had to be the woman herself . . . nobody else had had time to do such a thorough job.

And why no struggle? Okay, she was no Amazon. Okay, grant the fact that she might have been weak from lack of food. Okay, she was no spring chicken. But *something*. A bruise, a scratch . . . hell's teeth she didn't go to a particularly horrific death without making at least token resistance. Or if she did . . . *why*?

All questions which had to be answered before they started the murder enquiry proper. Because murder wasn't committed in a vacuum. It was a crime against a person — the ultimate crime against a person — and until the identity of that person was established, it was a little like groping around in an underground passage without light . . . and looking for a black cat you weren't even sure was there. The hit-and-miss quality was *that* monumental.

Blayde wasn't the worrying kind, nevertheless he knew his own position in the scheme of things to the last inch. He was the final can-carrier. Not Harris; Harris's job was to make sure that he (Blayde) carried the cans . . . and that they were topped up and spilling over. Not Tallboy; Tallboy had been a good jack, but now he was 'uniform', which meant he could walk away from the damn enquiry and nobody would blame him . . . not even Harris, who could usually find enough to chew the balls off anybody for anything.

Blayde was surprised to find himself worrying about the enquiry. 'It goes with the job.' How many times had he preached *that* basic truth to men who'd been fed up to the teeth with running like the clappers and getting nowhere? 'It goes with the job, lad. It's not like the loonies who write books say it's like. It's not even like the *textbooks* say it's like. It's rough and it stays rough . . . and if you ever thought otherwise, you were a mug for taking the number.'

Blayde leaned forward and switched on the car radio. From the twin speakers a blast of guitar-backed caterwauling filled the car.

As he flipped the knob back to 'off' he growled, 'At least I don't have to stand *that* bloody racket.'

By midday, Monday, October 20th the soul-destroying slog of the enquiry had got into its stride. The villagers were being milked of every gramme of information. An Express Message had been circulated throughout the force, and to neighbouring forces, alerting every copper within a hundred miles of the scene. But, even as Express Messages go, it was a very empty gesture. 'Known as 'Annie Miller'.' And, other than the time and mode of death, that was about all. A few hundred coppers scribbled the message into their notebooks, then forgot it . . . because there were damn-all enquiries they *could* make on the strength of such meagre information.

'Something.' Constable Stone almost pleaded with Philippa Holmes. 'Look, this is the first house. Somebody — some car — *must* have passed. Last week, sometime. They *must* have passed.'

'I don't spend my time staring from the window.'

Philippa Holmes was something of a snob; something of a 'tarty' snob, had you asked Stone. The wife of a self-employed accountant . . . to her that *meant* something. She was more than a little 'with it' and she didn't take kindly to a fat-gutted copper hinting that she minded other people's business. Her slightly-too-heavily-painted lips curled as she submitted herself to the implied insults. She was a good citizen — the wife of a man of some importance in the city of Bordfield — but she was damned if she was going to be intimidated by this gross oaf of a village bobby.

Stone said, 'You knew her. You must have known her.'

'Why do you assume that?'

'She was a neighbour.'

'I choose my friends carefully.'

'Dammit, she lived next-door-but . . .'

'Don't swear at *me*, constable!'

Stone gaped, closed his mouth then, in near-disbelief, said, 'She's dead — murdered — don't you *care*?'

'Not particularly.'

'You don't mean that,' gasped Stone.

'Look . . .' The lips curled again. 'She was a dirty old woman. Filthy. Obnoxious. Why should I . . .'

'Filthy?' Stone grabbed at the word, like a drowning man snatching for a spar.

'Filthy,' repeated Philippa Holmes. 'I've seen her. In that midden she called a garden. Down on her hands and knees, grubbing around searching for potatoes.'

'What potatoes?'

'Potatoes. Root crops. Worms, for all I know. I wouldn't be surprised.'

'Mrs Holmes.' Stone's tone could never be other than gruff, but he picked his words carefully. He wanted information and, if the only way to get information was to kow-tow a little to this silly, stuck-up little bitch, he was prepared to do *that*. He said, 'Grubbing about in the garden. Which part of the garden?'

'The back garden. I was in the bedroom one day, when . . .'

'Which day?'

'How do I know? I'm in the bedroom every day.'

'This last week?'

'No. A month ago . . . perhaps longer.'

'But she was . . . on her knees?'

'On all fours. For a few minutes I couldn't understand what she was doing.'

'But . . . potatoes?'

'I should think so. I didn't stay to see.'

'So, perhaps not potatoes?'

'I don't know. I didn't care then . . . I don't care now. I didn't like the woman.'

'You knew her, then?'

'I've already told you, I choose . . .'

'Missus, before you like *or* dislike somebody, you have to *know* 'em.'

'Don't be ridiculous.'

'Well, *haven't* you?'

'Constable, I don't know you – or want to know you – but I don't like you.'

'Aye.' Stone nodded, ponderously. 'Maybe you're right, missus. Come to think of it, I don't know *you*.'

From his bedroom the elder of the two killers took the call he'd placed from the Bordfield Railway Hotel to the address in Rudolph Square, Vienna. His companion remained near the reception desk and the telephone switchboard to ensure that curiosity had not triggered off eavesdropping.

It was merely an extra and unnecessary precaution. The conversation was not in English, nor did it make sense other than to the two speakers. It lasted for little more than ten minutes and, as the killer returned the receiver to its rest, he looked sad rather than afraid.

The younger of the two men entered the bedroom, and said, 'Well?'

'Mevagissey at two o'clock tomorrow,' sighed the elder man.

'Mevagissey?'

'The Cornish coast.'

'Then what?'

'Who knows?' The elder man made a tiny, palm-spreading gesture. He said, 'Pack our bags. I'll go pay the bill. Cornwall . . . it's a long way. A long drive.'

NINE

Helena Schnitzler may well have been a proud member of the BDM but, having spent the night in the arms of her virile branch leader, she could no longer boast about her 'maidenhood'. Secretly, she was a little afraid – even a little ashamed – his love-making had had the savage, near-rape quality of a rutting stag. But it was past and the dual pride of her family and the Nazi Youth Movement prevented her from showing other than shining-eyed satisfaction.

'You were good,' he smiled, as they ate breakfast. 'You will stay with me until your schooldays are finished, then we will find a position of trust for you.'

'My father might . . .'

'Forget your father,' he interrupted. 'He is old. Foolish. *We* are the new Germany. If he tries to make trouble . . .' Again, he smiled, but this time the smile held a cold certainty. 'We are taught to handle trouble.'

Walter Schnitzler tried to 'make trouble' two days later. He stopped the branch leader in the street, demanded the return of his daughter and, when the branch leader laughed in his face, stormed, 'You are mad. Mad! You and your whole generation. You feed on the stupid prattlings of a criminal who will be voted out of office within the year. You are louts. You think you are above the law. But, believe me, I will prove to you that you are *not*.'

That night Schnitzler's bookshop was put to the torch. It burned and was destroyed; was *allowed* to be destroyed, because the firefighters were unwilling to attend until it was too late.

And still Schnitzler fought.

'I will see Behr,' he stormed, and tears of frustration and anger ran down his sunken cheeks. 'Behr will put these animals where they belong. He knows me. He knows I am a God-fearing man. A good German. He will clean the streets of this — this scum.'

His wife and niece listened in silence. Such a sad and wretched silence. Perhaps because they were women — perhaps because, unlike Schnitzler, their lives had not been lived within the covers of books — they suspected the futility of his rage and his certainty that, because he was right, he would claim final victory. They hoped he was right. They even prayed for him. But they didn't expect their prayers to be answered.

Colonel Lothar Behr. The biggest landowner in the district. Onetime hero of the Kaiser's air force, and still a power to be reckoned with. A true Prussian; ramrod-backed, stern-faced, shaven-headed. A man of undoubted courage. A man who, without hesitation, would thrust his hand into the white heat of a furnace if, by so doing, he might uphold the dignity of his beloved Germany.

He listened to Schnitzler's story without interruption, without expression.

Then he said, 'Let her go, Schnitzler.'

'But, colonel, she is my daughter. She is . . .'

'Let her go.' Behr waved Schnitzler silent. 'Things are happening in this Fatherland of ours. Versailles is being repayed. This Austrian — this Hitler — is opening the eyes of the people. Who cares about his ridiculous politics? He is putting greatness back into Germany. The youth, the next generation, they will make the Fatherland *known* again. No longer will we be called 'The Defeated Nation'. I tell you, Schnitzler, this man is working miracles. Already the world is wondering. A little afraid, perhaps. And with cause.

'The fighting services? Versailles denied them to us, but this Nazi party. This party of the youth. They must be kept under control . . . of course they must. But they must be allowed to create a fighting nation again. The Army, the Navy, the Air Force. Schnitzler — I tell you — they have already torn up the Treaty of Shame. Quietly, and without fuss, they are working. Drilling. Training. Building. Had you a son, Schnitzler, you would be proud.'

'My daughter, colonel. They have . . .'

'You've lived too long with women and girls, Schnitzler. Between them, they have emasculated you. They have removed your balls. Be proud, man. Be glad that at least one of your brats puts her country before her family. Be honoured that you have contributed one small part to the future of the Fatherland.'

Herr Schnitzler returned home and began to die. His disease? No identifiable disease . . . merely that he no longer wanted to live.

In 1938 The Party provided a 'position' for Helena Schnitzler. She became an auxiliary, trainee nurse at the Hohenlychen Hospital. There she met and befriended a young woman of her own age. Irma Grese. And they, along with their contemporaries at the hospital, fell under the spell of Professor Karl Gebhardt.

TEN

'Rotting teeth don't go with gold caps.'

Detective Sergeant Reese grunted agreement. He watched the dental surgeon examine the dental chart Carr had had prepared, and waited.

The dental surgeon said, 'Upper jaw, left premolar. According to this badly decayed . . . a hole like the Mersey Tunnel. But next to it – the molar – gold capped. It doesn't make sense.'

'It doesn't make sense,' agreed Reese. 'That's why I'm here.'

They were in a tiny room leading from the surgery; the room into which the dental surgeon retreated between patients, while his assistant cleaned up and laid out the various instruments. The room into which the dental surgeon led visitors (like detective sergeants) who were there other than to lie back and open their mouths.

It was a warm and cosy room; wall-to-wall carpeted and with two deep armchairs and a glass-topped, knee-high table. The assistant tapped on the door, entered and placed a tray with tea and biscuits on the table. She closed the door firmly behind her as she left.

'A Jewess?' The dental surgeon dropped two lumps of sugar into a cup as he asked the question.

'That's what we think.' Reese helped himself to three lumps, then added, 'We could be wrong.'

'It's a thought.' The dental surgeon stirred his tea. 'We have a moderately large Jewish community here in Bordfield. Shopkeepers, businessmen . . . that sort of thing. The older end like gold, when they can afford it. The youngsters don't. They have more sense.'

Reese sipped his tea and looked a question.

'It's not the best filling. Not the best capping,' explained the dental surgeon. 'Modern dentistry doesn't need it. And it comes pricey.'

'An investment?' suggested Reese mildly.

'Have an extraction to get out of the red?' The dental surgeon chuckled. 'That's a bit drastic.'

'It helps, if you're mugged.' Reese was a very down-to-earth thinker. 'Better than carrying it around in your hip pocket.'

'These days?' The dentist grinned, but his tone carried wry truth. 'It's an open invitation to have your teeth kicked out.'

'She was in the mid-sixties.' Reese drew the conversation back onto its tracks.

'And . . .' The dental surgeon glanced at the dental chart. 'Hasn't taken care of her teeth for years.'

'Think she can be traced?' asked Reese bluntly.

'With *that*?' The dental surgeon moved his cup to indicate the dental chart.

Reese nodded.

'I assume,' said the dental surgeon, 'it's possible to find a needle in a haystack. Given time and patience . . . and if the needle's there.'

'It's been done.'

'Given somebody who visits a dentist at least *fairly* regularly.'

'And she didn't?'

'From that chart — I haven't seen the teeth themselves, but from that chart — not within the last ten years at least. A personal opinion? Not within the last *twenty* years. Teeth don't rot overnight. Not to *that* extent.'

Bill Harper couldn't help. God knows, he wanted to help, but he'd been squeezed dry of every last fact he knew about the dead woman. Nevertheless, he accepted the possibility that there might be something — some small detail — he could have failed to remember. He sat in his favourite armchair, in the farmhouse kitchen of the cottage attached to his three-acre smallholding. He'd delivered the milk for the day and, at about this time, he usually sprawled in front of the Aga stove, soaking up the warmth and enjoying a quiet nap. One of the few 'perks' he permitted himself. Forty winks, before he pulled Wellingtons onto his stockinged feet and went outside to feed the chickens and generally straighten things up before darkness.

Part of the strict routine he'd set himself. Especially in the winter months. To thaw out, with his feet on the thick cloth-clipped rug and the well-used armchair moulding itself to his body.

'Every day?' pressed the detective constable.

'Every day. Winter and summer. One pint.'
'She never took a holiday?'
'Not to my knowledge.'
'Just the one pint? It never varied?'
'Never varied.'
The D.C. scratched the back of his neck, then asked, 'For how long?'
'Since I took the round over. Three years . . . about.'
'How did she pay you?'
'Cash. Every Saturday morning.'
'So, you'd see her at least once a week?'
'No.' Bill Harper shook his head. 'She left it with the empty bottle. The exact amount . . . every Saturday morning.'
'The price of a pinta's altered during the last three years,' observed the D.C.
'I left *her* a note. She straightened up the following Saturday.'
'Hell's teeth!' The D.C. blew out his cheeks. 'That's a funny bloody way to run a business.'
'If they were all as good at paying . . .' Bill Harper grinned.
The D.C. groped around in his mind for other questions to ask. He'd have liked a break-through. Something . . . *anything*. It was a little like sifting a sea-shore for one grain of sand. Everybody had an answer for everything, and yet this potty old woman could live here, surrounded by the deaf, the dumb and the blind, and nobody knew from blazes who the hell she was or *what* the hell she was.

Mary Harper hurried into the kitchen, went to the wall-cupboard above the sink and took out a bottle of Dettol.
'Young Billy's grazed his knee,' she said. 'He *will* climb up and down walls.'
'Did *you* know her?'
'What?' Mary Harper paused, her free hand still holding the partly open door of the wall-cabinet.
'Annie Miller,' said the D.C. 'Did you know her at all?'
'No.'
'Look,' said the D.C. desperately, 'I don't mean whether you knew her well. Just . . . did you *know* her?'
'I can't think I've ever even met her.'

Mary Harper closed the wall-cupboard door and hurried from the kitchen, to do running repairs on her son's injured knee.

The D.C. didn't know what to do with his hands. He shoved them into his jacket pocket, then pulled them out again. He ran his fingers through his hair, rubbed the side of his nose, massaged the nape of his neck, drew the back of a hand across his mouth.

Jesus wept, it was stupid. More than that . . . it was almost *creepy*. A whole village — a pittling little village — and this old witch had lived there, damn near in the centre of things, and nobody seemed to have spoken to her. To have even *seen* her. As if the whole damn village was involved in some sort of conspiracy to know sweet F.A. after she'd been strung up, like a side of beef. It wasn't natural.

'I won't wear it,' growled the D.C. in a voice tinged with desperation.

'What?' Bill Harper looked up at him, a faint smile touching his lips.

'Three years. You must have seen her *sometime*.'

'A couple of times,' said Harper slowly.

'You've already said . . .'

'Not to speak to. Coming in from the back garden.'

'When?'

'Oh, I dunno.' Harper gave a tiny shrug of the shoulders. 'A few months ago. Once last year. She was in the back garden, when I delivered. She spotted me walking up the front path, then scurried into the house, through the back door.'

'Why should she do that?'

'Your guess is as good as mine.'

'Why do you *think* she did it?'

'I dunno.'

'Was she frightened of you?'

'Why should she be?'

'I'm asking. It *sounds* as if she was frightened of you.'

'What the hell? I'm the milkman . . . that's all.'

'Did you kill her?' It was one hell of a question to ask in a very conversational tone of voice but, as far as the D.C. was concerned, it was the only question left.

Bill Harper's eyes opened and his jaw dropped.

'*Did* you kill her?' The question was repeated, but in a tone which was almost a sigh of defeat.

'The hell . . . I *found* her.'

'Not quite correct.'

'As good as.'

'They often do,' murmured the D.C.

'Who?'

'Murderers.'

'What?'

' "Find" their victims . . . as good as.'

'Out!' Harper's voice was hoarse and angry, as he pushed himself out of the armchair.

'Cool it,' said the D.C. sadly.

'Out of this house, before I throw you out . . . *and* I mean it.'

'Okay.' The D.C. nodded understanding of Harper's anger. As he turned to leave, he added, 'But you'll be asked again. Maybe more than once . . . and by people who'll demand an answer.'

Banks. Lloyds, Midland, Yorkshire, Trustee, Barclays. The whole sack of 'em. Glorified money boxes, shrouded in secrecy. Piling up the loot — other people's money — and no questions asked or answered. It was a hard world; a hard world for coppers seeking something that *had* to be there. Okay, march in with a court order, all signed, sealed and tidy, and some degree of co-operation might — just *might* — be forthcoming. But no off-the-record-and-between-friends stuff. Not even on a murder enquiry. Not even when the copper nosing around carried the rank of detective chief superintendent.

Blayde wasn't in the best of tempers as he entered the swish premises of the Bordfield branch of Nat West. He'd been given too many brush-offs already. He expected another brush off, but the chance had to be taken.

The teller asked his name. Blayde gave it, along with his rank, and asked to see the manager. 'Immediately and privately, please.'

The teller promised she'd do her best and, even when she mentioned the manager's name, it didn't ring bells.

She came back to her position at the counter, smiled and said, 'If you'll take the lift, sir.' She leaned forward and pointed. 'Mr Morgan will see you in his office.'

'Thanks.'

At least it had been easier than in some of the other banks. The blasted manager *existed*; he wasn't some invisible creep locked away behind steel doors; he was get-at-able; he wasn't out on the nearest golf course, drumming up custom at the nineteenth hole.

Blayde was met at the lift by a very severely dressed young lady who said, 'Chief Superintendent Blayde? This way, please,' then chased ahead of him along the corridor, knocked on a door, opened the door, and announced, 'Chief Superintendent Blayde, Mr Morgan.'

Near-recognition dawned in both men's eyes almost before the door was closed.

Then Morgan rose from his chair behind the desk, walked round the desk, gripped Blayde's hand and pumped away as only men who have shared some very dicey moments, and haven't seen each other for a lifetime, can shake hands.

'Blayde.' Morgan made it a two-fisted grip. 'By all that's holy, Bob Blayde. I never thought . . .'

'Nor I.' Coppers who tended to tremble whenever Blayde came within hailing distance wouldn't have believed it. The grin which threatened to split Blayde's face into two halves. The gleam of friendship – and something more than friendship – in his eyes. 'My God! Taffy Morgan. I always said you were a lucky bastard . . . remember?'

'Do I remember.' Morgan waved a hand. 'Sit down, Bob. This calls for a small celebration.'

Blayde flopped into the chair facing the desk. Morgan opened the corner drinks cabinet and, without either asking or being told, poured two double whiskies and handed one to Blayde.

He said, 'To the next one to die,' and raised his glass.

'To the next one to die.'

There was a once-upon-a-time solemnity in the manner in which they sipped their drinks in that age-old fighting man's toast. Then, Morgan returned to his chair, placed his drink on the surface of his desk and leaned forward.

'Now, Bob.' He smiled. 'Nothing to do with the bad old days?'

'No.' Blayde moistened his lips with whisky.

'And — or so I'm told — immediate and urgent.'

'Annie Miller,' said Blayde bluntly. Then, before Morgan could speak, he continued, 'The old lady murdered at Rimstone. Very little money in the house. No documents — no bankbook or cheque book — but she must have had cash *somewhere*.'

'You think here?' fenced Morgan.

'I know. Confidentiality . . . all that stuff. But she must have had it *somewhere*.'

Morgan hesistated then, very gently, said, 'She had a current account.'

'Ah!' It was almost a sigh of relief.

'The name, the address.' Morgan pulled a face. 'I had to wait until somebody asked. I couldn't volunteer information . . . not at this stage.'

'But eventually?'

'We'd have tried to contact the next-of-kin. Through the police . . . obviously.'

'Can I ask questions?'

'Can *I* ask a question?' countered Morgan.

'Certainly.'

'Who's her next-of-kin?'

'Not a clue.' Blayde's mouth twisted a little. 'There was an inquest this morning. 'Known as Annie Miller'. It's something coroners don't like. But that's as far as we can go. We can't positively identify.'

'According to the newspaper . . .' began Morgan.

'I know.' Blayde waved a hand. ''Ritual murder' . . . all that garbage.'

'Is that what it is? Garbage?'

'I dunno.' Blayde scowled. 'That's the problem, Taffy. Nobody knows a damn thing.'

'If she was a Jewess . . .'

'We *think*.'

'As bad as that?' Morgan stretched out a hand, fingered down a toggle and spoke into the inter-office microphone-cum-speaker.

'Miss Banks. Get me the file and statements on Annie Miller. Then ask Mrs Hartley to come to my office.' A metallic female voice said, 'Yes, Mr Morgan,' and Morgan lifted his finger from the toggle.

'Don't buy yourself a fertiliser farm.' Blayde called himself a fool for giving the warning. This was a murder enquiry and, by the sound of things, the first possible break-through. Important . . . and yet, if it meant the man opposite him fielding trouble, *not* important. He growled, 'Now I know, I can get the necessary authority.'

'As I recall,' mused Morgan, 'It was D-Day, plus four. And if a certain Sergeant Blayde hadn't been a damn sight faster than me with his Sten gun . . .'

'The others . . .' began Blayde.

'What others?'

'The other bank managers. I've seen quite a few, and *not* been able to see quite a few. I just don't want you to . . .'

Very softly, Morgan said, 'Let me clear some of my overdraft, Bob.'

'What overdraft?'

'Oh — lemme see — about forty years of life. A wife. Two kids. A nice house. A . . .'

'He could have missed,' grunted Blayde.

'At that range?' Morgan chuckled. 'Even *you* couldn't miss.'

Blayde left it at that. He sipped whisky and waited. That war . . . it had been a lousy war. Necessary, perhaps, but no less evil. Sergeants Blayde and Morgan had struck up a friendship and, because of that friendship, the war had been a little less intolerable. Two youngsters, full of spit and vinegar; good enough to carry chevrons on their sleeves. Good enough. Ruthless enough. Mad enough to kill other youngsters, equally full of spit and vinegar. War. No goodies, no baddies. Just youngsters in different dress and if the other guy wore the style you'd been told to shoot holes into . . . hard luck for the guy inside the cloth.

'It was bloody mad,' muttered Blayde.

Morgan nodded. Without further explanation he knew exactly what Blayde meant.

The woman, Mrs Hartley, brought the file and statements. Having received a tiny nod of approval from Morgan she answered Blayde's questions. Yes, she knew Mrs Miller. 'She always came to my counter. She'd wait in a queue, rather than go to any of the other tellers.' Why was that? 'She was an elderly lady — not *old*, but getting on a bit — and she had her peculiar foibles.' She cashed cheques, did she? 'Yes, about once a month, thereabouts. She always left her cheque book at the bank, though.' She left her cheque book at the bank? 'Yes. And her credit book. Her 'putting in' book as she called it.' A bit unusual, wasn't it?

'Not really.' Morgan answered the question. 'Some people — especially elderly people — seem scared of cheques. They dislike the idea of carrying a cheque book around with them. Of having it in the house, even. They think it might be stolen and, whoever steals it, might cash cheques. Take all the money they have. Even land them in debt.'

'Was there a pattern to the cashing of cheques?'

'Not really.' Mrs Hartley answered the question. She glanced over Morgan's shoulder to check the statements. 'About once a month. And always a hundred pounds. Never more. Never less.'

'She carried a hundred pounds around with her . . . but not her cheque book?'

'That's what it boils down to.' Morgan nodded.

'When did she last cash a cheque?'

'A month — just over a month ago.' Morgan glanced at the statement. 'September seventeenth.' He consulted his desk calendar. 'That was on a Wednesday.'

'I remember. I cashed the cheque, after I'd made it out and she'd signed it,' said Mrs Hartley. 'I remember Mr Bryant — that's another teller — his counter position was empty, and I was busy with one of the shopkeepers. He was banking-in. Mr Bryant called for her, but she insisted on waiting.'

Yes; Mrs Hartley had passed the time of day with the murdered woman; not long conversations, of course, but the usual pleasantries which pass between the staff of a bank and customers. Yes; she *had* seen Mrs Miller other than in the bank; twice, perhaps three times, she'd passed her on the streets of Bordfield; shopping; each time she'd been weighed down by large shopping-bags, which seemed to be full of food.

'Shopping,' mused Blayde.

Morgan said, 'It's not *so* unusual. Bordfield's one of the main shopping areas round these parts.'

'It's no small distance from Rimstone.'

'There's a through train service,' explained Morgan. 'Beechwood Brook to Bordfield. It stops at Rimstone. A train every hour . . . thereabouts. A pick-up for the London trains. Some of the staff live at Beechwood Brook. They use it.'

Blayde returned his attention to the woman. Yes; she (Mrs Hartley) realised that Mrs Miller hadn't been English; her English was easily understandable, but the foreign accent had been there; guttural, that was the best way to describe it. Jewish? Well, perhaps, but she (Mrs Hartley) had a sister-in-law who was a Jewess, and her English was perfect; Mrs Miller *could* have been a Jewess but, if so, not an English Jewess; continental perhaps . . . *if* she was a Jewess.

'You seem to have some doubts,' said Blayde gently.

'No.' She smiled and shook her head. 'I just don't know. She was not English . . . that I *do* know. But — y'know — Jewish? How could anybody tell?'

'A hundred quid a time?' said Blayde.

'In five pound notes,' said the woman.

'From where?'

'From here. This bank. From her current account.'

'So, she must have put in. Topped up.'

'She was never in the red.' Morgan flipped the pages of statements. 'Fifteen hundred, September twenty-sixth. That was a Friday. Tuesday, April seventeenth, twelve hundred. Last year, November twentieth, a round thousand. All deposits. That's how it goes on. Right back to when she became a customer, about twelve years ago. It was always topped up. Round figures. And always withdrawn in hundreds.'

'Cash,' murmured Mrs Hartley.

Blayde looked at her.

'Cash,' she repeated. 'She paid in in cash . . . usually used ten pound notes. She withdrew in cash. Always twenty five pound notes.'

'And . . .' Morgan glanced at the statements. 'Her present balance, in credit. Four thousand five hundred pounds.'

Blayde pursed his lips in a silent whistle.

By ten o'clock that night (Monday, October 20th) the leg-weary P.B.I. of the enquiry had dictated their reports and statements into microphones at the Incident Centre, prior to staggering off home, putting their feet up and watching how television cops solve multiple murder in sixty minutes flat. The strange thing: real-life policemen tend to form the bulk of the regular viewers of this everlasting stream of forensic crap. Often to criticise. 'Holy cow! If I drove a police car like that, they'd make me pay for the bloody thing.' Or, 'Will you look at *that*? He's just had blue shit kicked out of him, and he isn't even *marked*.'

The wives and teenage children of working policemen develop the knack of stopping their ears to such remarks. It's only the old man showing off; by implication telling the world in general how much better *he* can bobby.

Coincidentally, Blayde was making a remark about television sets.

'Four-and-a-half thousand quid,' he said, 'and look at that house. Look how she lived. Not even a goggle-box. Not even a transistor.'

'Not even a newspaper delivery,' added Tallboy.

Two typists had been drafted to the Incident Centre, in order to listen to tapes, on headphones, and translate what they were hearing into neatly typed, properly paragraphed and reasonably well punctuated English. The clack and ring of the typewriters formed a background to the quiet talk of Blayde and Tallboy. It was what the less polite members of the constabulary called a 'gum session'; a squirrel-cage of conversation, without beginning and without end. A reluctance to allow the enquiry to free-wheel into another day. A nagging doubt (and that doubt is always there) that somebody, somewhere, had missed that vital hint which could turn a murder hunt into a positive direction.

The door of the village hall opened, and the vicar's wife entered, carrying two king-sized Thermos jugs.

'Who's she?' asked Blayde, *sotto voce*.

'The parson's wife.'

'What's she doing in here?'

'She's a thriller buff.'

'Oh, my Christ,' breathed Blayde. 'That's *all* we need.'

'Hot soup,' proclaimed the vicar's wife, as she plonked one of the Thermos jugs on the table, between the two typists. She walked across the room to Blayde and Tallboy, and said, 'Hot soup, gentlemen. I'm sure you're in need of it.'

'Madam . . .' began Blayde.

'Just the job.' Tallboy smiled and interrupted whatever Blayde was going to say.

'I've been thinking . . .' She unstoppered the jugs and poured two plastic beakers to the brim with steaming soup, as she talked. 'I've been thinking . . . about this murder . . .'

Blayde sighed, heavily.

'Well, not exactly about the murder, more about Mrs Miller. I think you're wrong. I don't think she was a Jewess.'

'No?' Blayde showed some mild interest. He reached for one of the beakers, drew his fingers from its side, hurriedly, then said, 'Damn!'

'It's very hot.' The warning came too late. Blayde shook out a clean handkerchief, folded it and used it to protect his fingers as he lifted the beaker to his mouth. The vicar's wife continued, 'No, I don't think she was Jewish. I think she was German.'

Tallboy performed the handkerchief trick, tasted the soup and smiled his approval.

Blayde said, 'German?'

'When we first came here,' she explained. 'This is my husband's first parish and — you know how it is — the new parson's wife and the ladies of the village — I trotted around to let them all see me. That I had a limb at each corner, and only one head . . . the usual thing.'

'German?' Blayde didn't want any wandering from the point.

'Yes — well — Mrs Miller was in her garden. Actually, I was calling on Mrs Henderson — she lived next door to Mrs Miller — she doesn't now, the Hendersons moved out about three years ago and the . . .'

'German?' repeated Blayde grimly.

'Ah, yes.' The vicar's wife smiled. 'Well, it was a lovely day, you see. And I was with Mrs Henderson — in the garden — and I saw Mrs Miller in *her* garden. Over the dividing hedge. And I called out to her . . . and she said *'Mein Gott!'*.'

'*Mein Gott?*'

'Quite distinctly. I think I surprised her. In fact I'm *sure* I surprised her. She just said, '*Mein Gott!*' and ran indoors.'

'And later?' pressed Blayde.

'What?'

'Later? When you spoke to her later?'

'Oh, I didn't. I called. I wanted to apologise for frightening her, but she wouldn't answer the door.'

'You've never seen her since? Is that what you're saying?'

'I've seen her. I haven't *spoken* to her . . . or to be strictly accurate, she hasn't spoken to *me*.'

'Ignored you?'

'In effect.'

'How long is this since?' asked Tallboy.

'What?'

'Since you startled Mrs Miller in her garden?'

'Well, we've been here seven years. It was shortly after we arrived.'

'Seven years ago?'

'Yes.' She nodded. 'I mean . . . I couldn't even telephone to tell her how sorry I was. She hasn't a phone. And I must have called at least a dozen times over the years. At *least* a dozen times. And I'm sure she was in, more than once. She just wouldn't answer when I rang the doorbell.'

It was almost midnight; almost a new day. Blayde drove the Fiesta towards his home at a steady, moderate speed; at a speed which needed no real concentration. The wipers were on intermittent in order to clear the windscreen of the dampness of the October night. Overhead the clouds scudded across the face of a moon which hadn't quite reached full. It was a pleasant enough night for October. A night for memories of similar nights; similar drives home in the darkness, mid-way through a major crime enquiry. Similar nights, on the continent of Europe, when the khaki flood had rolled back the field-grey armies of a madman; when each dawn brought the near-certain promise of a sight never to be forgotten. Bad days, sad days . . . but at the same time glorious days. Taffy Morgan. Other men — dozens of 'em — closer, for the moment, than any brother could ever be. And the promises. Never to lose touch. Ever! Life-long friendships, sworn in the smoke-filled atmosphere of some bistro. And they'd been meant. Not empty promises. Despite the red biddy — the almost lethal concoctions they downed in order to fight off the nightmares — honourable men making promises which, at the time, they had no intention of ever breaking.

Crap, of course.

Who the hell ever kept those promises? Once out of uniform, who the hell ever *wanted* to keep them? To stir those other memories? To recreate the horrors? Never able to even *try* to forget?

It had been nice bumping into Taffy Morgan in that way. Nice . . . and convenient. A fistful of photostats which, had it been anybody other than Taffy, he wouldn't have had a snowball's chance of getting.

So, okay, war had its uses . . . in a very devious way. It threw future bank managers and future detective chief superintendents together, and solved yet-to-be-committed murders.

Maybe . . .

He pulled into the drive of his cottage, garaged the car, then let himself into the one place on earth in which he could really relax. As he kicked off his shoes and loosened his tie the cat rubbed a welcome home against the side of his leg.

He bent down, scratched that spot between its ears which turned the purring on to full blast.

He said, 'Cat, we'll come to an arrangement. Next time round, I'll be you and *you* can taste the joys of sorting out a particularly lousy world.'

'A Jewess or a German,' mused Tallboy.

'Or,' contributed Susan, 'a German Jewess.'

'Yeah.'

Tallboy had bathed, changed into pyjamas and dressing-gown and had joined his wife on the rug, in front of the glowing electric fire. They were sipping hot chocolate. Susan Tallboy was also in her night clothes and wearing a quilted dressing-gown. Without makeup and with her hair brushed and gleaming in the reflection from the red-hot bars, to Tallboy she looked as beautiful as she'd ever looked.

The years hadn't hardened her in any way. She was a woman loved and, as with all such women, the inner glow of eternal youth mocked the passing of time. The only illumination came from the fire, and the room was a comfortable cave of scarlet and black; a cave of security and warmth. And Tallboy found himself wishing that the whole world might be as lucky and as content as he was at that moment.

He tasted his chocolate, then said, 'Such a strange woman. So obviously unhappy. Out of touch with *everything*.'

'The impression . . .' Susan leaned back and rested her head on her husband's lap. 'D'you want to hear my impression?'

'Of course.'

'That she was frightened. Terrified. So frightened that she'd opted out. Built a wall of secrecy around herself. A thick, broad wall, which included the village. At Bordfield – at the bank, when she did her shopping – that was the only time she ventured outside that wall. No telephone, no radio, no television, not even newspapers. She didn't want to *know*. Something . . . Some memory from the past terrified her.'

'Waiting,' murmured Tallboy.

'What?'

Tallboy sipped his drink, then repeated, 'Waiting. That's the impression *I* get. The wall of secrecy . . . sure, I go along with that. But she was comparatively rich. Somewhere she had money – stored away – and she used it to keep the bank supplied. Frightened? Okay, frightened. But she could have been frightened in comfort. I think she was waiting. She didn't want the comfort. She didn't need it. Maybe she thought it would have been wasted.'

'Because she was waiting?'

'Uhuh.' Tallboy nodded.

'For what?'

'To be murdered,' said Tallboy softly. Slowly. 'She knew it was coming. She just didn't know when. So she was . . . waiting.'

ELEVEN

Professor Karl Gebhardt. A fine surgeon; the world recognised him as a fine surgeon; one of the great surgeons of his era. That in June of 1948 he was executed at Landsberg because of the horrors he had perpetrated in the name of 'scientific advancement' can never alter the fact that his skill with the scalpel was unsurpassed.

With charity it might be said that *because* he was such an outstanding surgeon he was doomed to be executed. Had he been a mere jack-booted lemming, following the orders of his superiors, he might have escaped the hangman's noose. But he was a surgeon – a great surgeon – *and* a schoolboy friend of Heinrich Himmler *and* a fanatical National Socialist *and* a fervent advocate of the doctrine of 'The Master Race'. The combination cost him his life.

But in 1938, at Hohenlychen Hospital, Gebhardt was a god, and worshipped as such. Helena Schnitzler and Irma Grese were merely two of his devoted followers. He could do no wrong, and proof of his impeccable party purity was to be found in the periodic visits to the hospital by top Nazi officials. Heydrich, Hess, Streicher. They all put themselves into the hands of Gebhardt, and they were all his friends.

By 1939 the Hohenlychen Hospital was geared to repair the war wounded. The heroes of the Fatherland; the Waffen SS; the elite troups of Hitler's armies and the heroes of Helena and her colleagues.

Gebhardt and his team performed near-miracles of surgery, and part of that team were Helena and Irma. They took wounds which only war can inflict and, in effect, rebuilt men from broken pieces. But still Gebhardt wasn't satisfied; still he sought answers; still he drove his team to the point of utter exhaustion in an attempt to harness medicine and surgery to total war.

'Infections. Gangrene,' he stormed. 'The flower of our armies are beyond real repair before they even reach Hohenlychen. They arrive too late. Their flesh is already rotting. There must be a way . . . there *must* be a way.'

He and his team sought that 'way' at a nearby concentration camp called Ravensbrück.

It was such a pathetic little funeral. Frau Schnitzler walked slowly away from the grave; from the cemetery on the rise beyond the village. For long she had wondered what it would be like to be a widow. As Walter had gradually forced his body to die, she had wondered. Now she knew. It was no different. Walter was dead . . . but in effect Walter had *been* dead for such a long time. Since Helena had left. He had watched the rise of the party as from a distance. As from a being from some other planet. The victories — the so-*called* victories — had failed to touch him. Poland and the declaration of war . . . his eyes had remained dull and without real interest.

It would be no great hardship, no great *difference*, being a widow.

Hannah said, 'Helena should have been with us.'

'She was told.' It was a flat, hard statement of fact. An accusation.

'The message might not have reached her.'

'It reached her.' Frau Schnitzler's lips moved into an ugly curl of scorn. 'She was right not to come. It would have been a blasphemy.'

They walked in silence. The elder woman dry-eyed and stern-faced. The younger woman with lines of extra sadness etched into her expression. They were watched, but the watchers pretended not to see. These were dangerous times. It was unwise to show compassion; to make an outward display of sympathy to those who openly opposed the present authority.

As they crossed the tiny square of the village two men walked towards them. The taller of the men slipped a hand into the inside pocket of his jacket and produced the pasteboard upon which their authority was based. They blocked the path of the two women.

'Hannah Muller?' The taller man held his card of identification for the two women to see.

'My niece,' said Frau Schnitzler and, for a moment, held a protective arm across the shoulders of the younger woman.

'Hannah Muller?'

The question was repeated. The voice was bored, almost tired, and the man ignored the elder woman.

'I am Hannah Muller.'

'With us, please.'

The taller man glanced at a car parked in a street off the square. The shorter man put out a hand and grasped Hannah's arm; the grip was not hard or hurtful, but merely a guidance and a gentle underlining of authority.

Frau Schnitzler watched them walk towards the parked car.

TWELVE

'Something . . .' Tallboy sought the appropriate word, then plumped for 'foul. Something creepy. Not a run-of-the-mill murder.'

'Are any of 'em?' Blayde refused to be drawn.

They stood a yard or two from the entrance to the village hall; giving the arriving officers plenty of room in which to arrive at the Incident Centre without necessarily having to acknowledge the presence of the two chief superintendents. Another instance of practical policing. To let the rankers know that the weight was around, but without treading on coat-tails. An implied gesture of reliance.

Anyway, despite the odd spot or two of rain, it was fresher, cleaner out here in the open. Inside, despite the newly opened windows, the fug of the night's smoking hadn't yet cleared. The clerks, assisted by a couple of drafted in policewomen, were busy sorting and cross-referencing the statements and reports compiled by the all-night typists. The paperwork. Always the paperwork. Yards of the infernal stuff. All entered in the makeshift card indexes . . . and all adding up to damn-all.

'The way she was killed,' pressed Tallboy.

'Kinky,' agreed Blayde. 'The world's stiff with kinky bastards.'

'The German/Jew business.'

'She was foreign. Probably continental. *Maybe* a Jewess.'

'Her age.'

'Around the sixty mark. Maybe sixty-five.'

'Her life-style. She was a hermit.'

'It's not yet illegal.'

'Bob, you're being deliberately awkward,' accused Tallboy.

'Devil's advocacy.' Blayde smiled. 'Chris, you're right, *maybe* you're right. But one day, with luck, some animal's going to be standing in a dock. And he'll be defended. And all the things *you've* said? They don't mean a damn thing.'

'First catch your hare,' murmured Tallboy.

'Touché.'

'That money.' Tallboy came down to earth. 'She puts it in. She takes it out. She gets it from *somewhere*.'

'I know . . . *where*?'

'Stocks and shares, perhaps?'

'I doubt it.' Blayde didn't quite dismiss the idea out of hand. 'No telephone. I can't see anybody playing the stock market without a telephone.'

'A good broker?'

'Possible.' Blayde moved his shoulders. 'It's a line. It needs following.'

The talk continued for another ten minutes or so. Empty, groping talk. Questions without answers and answers without substance. They both knew the truth of the game; that frustration, too, is part of any murder enquiry. Blayde had struck oil at the bank, and a question had been answered. But the answer had posed an even bigger question. The problem — the *real* problem — to get inside the mind of the murdered woman. To think as she thought. To know the fears she knew.

The rain grew heavier, and they sought shelter in the Incident Centre.

Kelly left one of the trestle-tables and walked over to them. He spoke to Blayde.

'The back garden, sir.'

Blayde waited.

'A report from Stone,' said Kelly. 'Another report from one of the jacks who interviewed the milkman. She seems to have spent some time in the back garden.'

'It was her own garden.'

'Grubbing about, according to a Mrs Holmes.'

'Grubbing about?' Blayde showed some interest.

'Constable Stone interviewed her. She wasn't too co-operative.'

'Wasn't she, now?'

'Pretty well ordered him out of the house, before he could press for more detail.'

'Where does she live?' asked Tallboy.

'Next door to the scene. No . . .' Kelly corrected himself. 'Next door but one to the scene. First house on the left.'

'I wonder,' mused Tallboy, 'if she'll order *me* out of the house?'

Rowe, too, was 'mucking in'. By nine o'clock he was at the local council offices asking about rate demands and how Annie Miller made payment. By nine-thirty he was at the local branch of the North Eastern Electricity Board making similar enquiries. Both answers were the same. Personally, and in cash. No cheques, and no delay in payment. And when the electricity meter was read? 'As I understand it, there's a garage attached to the house. That's where the meter is. The garage isn't locked. The meter reader calls, takes the reading and doesn't bother with the occupant. It's standard when we can get to the meter without bothering the customer.'

'Can you check that?'

'Eh?'

'From the meter reader. Just to be sure.'

'Oh, aye. I'll verify. But I'm almost sure.'

'Let me know if he ever did go inside. If he'd ever seen the woman.'

'I'll do that. He's out at the moment.'

'When he gets back.'

'I'll have a word. If he can help I'll be in touch.'

Inspector Rowe would have liked to help. He'd have liked to detect the murder. Not for himself . . . for Tallboy. A new divisional officer. 'Murder — Undetected' didn't look good within weeks of taking on the rank. And Tallboy deserved to look good, because Tallyboy *was* good. A good copper and a fine man. Come to that, Blayde wasn't in anybody's debt, either. Tougher, harder than Chris Tallboy, but a man it was a pleasure to work under. Tallboy and

Blayde — Blayde and Tallboy — it didn't matter how you permutated the names . . . one hell of a team.

Rowe felt at peace with the world as he pushed open the swing doors of Sopworth Police Station. For a moment he hardly noticed the man at the public counter, then certain words impinged themselves on his ears.

'. . . Rowe. Harry Rowe. That's the man I wanna see.'

'If you mean Inspector Rowe . . .' P.C. Higginbottom glanced past the man's shoulder and at the newly arrived section officer.

'That's what *you* have to call him. But to me he's . . .'

'To you he's what?' asked Rowe coldly.

'Eh?'

The stranger spun round. He was a short man; short, busy, plump and pompous. His grey hair was cut short and its colour emphasised the florid features; the bulbous nose; the cobweb of tiny veins which covered the slightly bloated face. The impression was one of booze; years of booze which had heightened his colour, broadened his waistline and befuddled his brain. The clothes went with the man; a light grey, large-patterned suit, brown shoes and a yellow tie against a blue shirt.

He held out a hand and said, 'Harry!'

Rowe used his hands to peel off his gloves.

'Harry,' said the fat man. 'You remember me. Billy Caldwell.'

'No,' said Rowe flatly.

'C'mon . . . we were at school together. Remember?'

'No, I don't remember.' Rowe removed his peaked cap and placed his gloves inside it before he positioned the cap carefully on the public counter. He pretended not to notice Higginbottom's sly grin. He snapped, 'The name's Rowe. The rank's inspector. And I don't take kindly to strangers talking to my men as if they're my long lost uncle.'

Higginbottom's face straightened. The fat man scowled.

'Your business?' demanded Rowe.

'Well, if that's how you . . .'

'State your business.'

'Okay, okay, it's about our lass.'

'Who's that?'

'Annie. Annie Caldwell. Married Bert Miller. Now he's done her in. That's my 'business', mister bloody Inspector Rowe.'

Higginbottom let out his breath in a long, silent whistle. Rowe stared at the fat man for a moment, before he spoke.

'Annie Miller?' he said.

'That's who.'

'You claim she's your sister?'

'Nothing less. She came to live in these parts.'

'From where?'

'Preston . . . just outside Preston.'

'And she was married to somebody called Miller?'

'Albert Miller. A real bastard if ever one lived.'

'When?' asked Rowe.

'Eh?'

'When did she leave Preston? When was the last time you saw her?'

'Happen five years back. Happen nearer six. We haven't clapped eyes on each other since.'

Rowe picked his cap and gloves from the counter.

He said, 'No more questions for the moment, Caldwell. First stop the public morgue.'

'Aye.' Caldwell nodded eager agreement.

'Then, if you can give us a positive identification . . .'

The younger of the two killers was driving the car. The elder had a road map of Devon and Cornwall spread out on his knee.

The elder man said, 'Keep to the M5. Then make for Okehampton.'

'Look, what can they do to us?' The younger man's worry had increased to near-panic proportions.

'Take the A30.' The elder man's tone was unruffled.

'We did what we had to do, that's all.'

'We did what we had to do.' The elder man's voice was both calm and calming. As he traced the roads on the map with his finger, he asked, 'That being so, why couldn't you sleep last night?'

'It wasn't a good hotel. The bed wasn't comfortable.'

'One of the best hotels in Bristol,' murmured the elder man.

'The bed wasn't comfortable.'

'Or your conscience.' The elder man smiled sadly.

'Look, if you think...'

'I *saw* those places.' Still, the elder man studied the road map as he talked. In a kindly, paternal voice he said, 'To be told. But to *live*. There is a great difference, my friend.' Then almost without pause, 'From Okehampton on the A30. Then to St Austell. We should see signs to Mevagissey.'

'Why Mevagissey?' The younger man's voice was petulant.

'It's a port.' The elder man began to re-fold the road map. 'Plymouth has an airport. Too many people would like to know The Hunter's movements.'

'The Hunter!' The younger man's voice held mild contempt.

'It's a name.' The elder man stored the road map away. 'He follows trails. He hunts. What other name would you have him use?'

Rowe pulled back the sheet. The morgue stank, as only a mortuary not equipped with deep-freeze drawers can stink. Cleanliness (and the Sopworth public mortuary was clinically clean) can not ease, or even slow down, putrefaction. Therefore, the morgue stank; the sweet, sickly smell of flesh slowly going rotten. Rowe had known what to expect. Caldwell hadn't; Caldwell had had visions of filing-cabinet drawers, ready to be pulled out on smooth-sliding runners. Instead, there was the slab beneath triple strip-lighting; the ceiling-high white tiles; the stainless steel sink with double draining board; the glass-fronted cabinet showing scalpels, knives, tiny hammers, chisels and a small saw. Rowe had flipped on the light and walked straight to the sheeted corpse.

'Well?' Rowe snapped the question.

Caldwell was still at the door. He seemed unwilling to move nearer to the slab.

'You're here to say 'Yes' or 'No',' said Rowe.

'Gimme – gimme a minute.' Caldwell moistened his lips.

'If it's your sister...'

'I dunno. From here... I dunno.'

'From there's no damn good. I want you here. Near enough to be sure.'

'I...' Caldwell rubbed his mouth; seemed to be trying to massage life back into his lips. He groaned, 'I wanna find her. That's all. Since she left . . .' He shook his head. 'I wanna *find* her.'

'Annie Miller?'

Caldwell nodded.

'This is Annie Miller,' said Rowe. 'We have to know if it's *your* Annie Miller.'

'We're — we're not Jews.' Caldwell sought excuses. 'The papers... they said a Jewess. She wasn't . . .'

'Positive or negative,' insisted Rowe. 'There *has* to be an identification.

'Harry, for God's sake . . .'

'Don't call me 'Harry'.' Rowe's voice was harsh with impatience and annoyance. 'I don't remember you. Maybe we were at the same school, I don't know. Just come closer. Look!'

Caldwell closed his eyes for a moment. He opened them, took a deep breath of the sweet-sickly air then forced his legs to carry him nearer to the slab. He stood alongside Rowe and stared, wide-eyed at the face of the dead woman.

'Well?' asked Rowe.

Caldwell shook his head.

'It's not your sister?'

'No. It's not . . .'

Caldwell's legs buckled and he dropped, untidily onto the tiled floor alongside the slab. Rowe re-arranged the sheet over the face of the corpse, bent and, with a hand hooked under each armpit, dragged Caldwell into the open air. He left him propped against the wall while he locked the mortuary door.

Caldwell opened his eyes and was immediately violently sick.

Rowe waited, then said, 'Not your sister?'

'No.' Caldwell pushed himself unsteadily to his feet. 'Christ . . . I musta passed out.'

'It happens.'

'What — what do I do now?'

'Nothing.' Rowe moved a hand. 'Go back home. Keep looking for your sister presumably.'

'Aye.' Caldwell nodded dumbly.

Rowe said, 'Of course . . . she might not want you to find her.'

Cockburn said, 'Piano wire? Assuming I wanted to buy some, where would I go?'

Police Sergeant 1871 William Henry Cockburn was in Lessford. He'd travelled farther afield than his colleagues. This for two reasons. In the first place, piano wire was a very specialised product; it wasn't for sale at the nearest corner shop; it wasn't part of the stock of electrical contractors. It seemed, therefore, that piano wire might only be available in a large city. Like Bordfield. Like Lessford. But (Cockburn's second reason) Joe Lodge — *Professor* Joseph Lodge — didn't live in Bordfield. He lived in Lessford, and had his shop at Lessford, and it had been *years* . . .

Cockburn was no mean pianist. No Paderewski, you understand. No Oscar Peterson. But he could tickle the old ivories when the spirit moved him; he could hammer out a singalong with the best. And — way and gone to hell in his jazz-orientated youth — Joe Lodge (*Professor* Joseph Lodge) had been one of his music teachers. Not the best teacher, but by far the most colourful teacher. Lodge ran a shop on the fringe of the city centre; one of the few genuine *music* shops in the North. Not for him records, guitars or, indeed, instruments of any kind. Joseph Lodge — self-styled 'professor' — dealt in the dots . . . period. The printed music itself. He was over the ears in the stuff. The window of the shop was crammed with sheet music. The interior was like a library, with every shelf crammed with the stuff and (supposedly) all carefully filed and catalogued. And — okay, accepting that it wasn't *quite* as systematically shelved as it might have been — where else, outside London, could you buy just about anything and everything from the piano score of *Alice Where Art Thou* — with variations — up past the standard big-band arrangement of *String of Pearls* to the whole shooting match for orchestra and performers of Beethoven's *Choral*.

There was a back room to the shop. Cockburn and Lodge were in that room and, as they talked, Cockburn sipped rum-laced coffee.

'Piano wire.' Cockburn tried to ease the thin end of the conversational wedge into Lodge's everlasting mutterings.

'This.' Lodge waved a dramatic arm which enveloped the scattered piles of manuscript which spilled from the top of the concert grand which, in turn, just about filled the room. Then his voice dropped to its previous mumbling as he squiggled marks with a felt-tipped pen on the sheet of manuscript propped before him on the piano. 'Mahler. His Resurrection Symphony. This utter rubbish he called 'progressive tonality'. Ironing the kinks out . . . that's what I'm doing . . .'

'Piano wire.'

'. . . a touch of Mendelssohn here, a hint of Mozart there . . . give 'em a *tune* to listen to . . .'

'Piano wire.'

'. . . for two pianos — a piano duet. That's why the damn thing's so rarely performed. Too expensive . . . too many players. Two pianos and some melody. Something pleasant . . .'

'Prof . . .' Cockburn almost shouted, *'Piano wire*!'

'Eh?' Lodge lowered his pen, and stared. 'You want to buy some?'

'You sell it?' Cockburn's expression was one of surprise.

'Sell what?'

'Piano wire?'

'Good god, no. Why should I sell piano wire? Who's likely to want to buy . . .'

'Where *could* I buy it?' pressed Cockburn.

'I'll get some for you. When will you be round here again?'

'Prof.' Cockburn loved this old eccentric, much as a man might love a slightly gaga uncle. He said, 'There's an old lady been murdered out at Rimstone . . .'

'Indeed? Why should you want to buy piano . . .'

'Whoever killed her used piano wire.'

'Oh!'

'He must have bought it from somewhere.'

'Not from here. I don't sell . . .'

'No, I'm not suggesting he bought it from you. I want to know where he might have bought it.'

'A piano manufacturer — a piano repairer — where else?'

'Sure, but . . .'

'Or, somebody who wants to get rid of some ancient instrument. You can sometimes find broken down pianos on council tips. They aren't the instruments they used to be. Japanese pianos . . . whoever heard of *Japanese* pianos? The Germans, William. The only nation ever to make a really *good* piano. Good God, a piano isn't a motor cycle. How can a nation renowned for making . . .'

'How many piano makers?' interrupted Cockburn.

'Eh?'

'Here in Lessford. How many piano makers? How many piano repairers?'

'They don't *make* them, William. They *assemble* them. The component parts are shipped over from . . .'

'Germany, I know.' Cockburn nodded. 'But how many? Makers and repairers?'

'Two in Lessford. Makers. Although I wouldn't call one of them a 'maker'. More of a 'dealer'. I doubt if they could . . .'

'And repairers?'

'One . . . just the one.'

'So, if I wanted to buy some piano wire . . .'

'Try the tuners,' suggested Lodge.

'Eh?' This time it was Cockburn's turn to stare.

'All the tuners carry some around with 'em. All the tuners worth calling tuners.'

'How many tuners?' asked Cockburn weakly. 'Here and at Bordfield?'

'God knows. Scores. Hundreds, perhaps. Frustrated pianists mostly. Frustrated composers. Half of 'em shouldn't be allowed within a hundred yards of a decent piano. I wouldn't let 'em . . .'

'Jesus Christ!' breathed Cockburn.

'What?'

'I thought I'd picked up the *easy* chore. Piano wire. Builders, makers, repairers, dealers, tuners, even council tips. We're up to the knees in bloody piano wire.'

'I wouldn't say that. *Good* piano wire. That's not . . .'

'Good or bad. As long as it forms a noose.'

'William.' Lodge gazed solemnly at his former pupil. 'Remember what I used to say? 'Perfection, nothing less.' It doesn't matter what you want it for. Always the best. It's cheapest in the long run.'

'I am,' said Tallboy with cool correctness, 'a police chief superintendent. I am the divisional officer of Beechwood Brook. That means I am the senior officer in charge of this whole division.'

'Really?' Philippa Holmes raised carefully pencilled eyebrows in a slightly amused, slightly sardonic response.

'I understand,' continued Tallboy, 'that you declined to allow one of my officers to pursue this enquiry.'

'Really?' The eyebrows were raised a fraction higher.

'This officer.' Tallboy moved a hand to indicate the rather embarrassed P.C. Stone.

The immaculate painted lips curled.

'A murder enquiry,' said Tallboy gently.

'He asked me questions. I answered them.'

'Not completely. Not all of them.'

'As many as I could answer.'

'Not even that.'

'I think you're being slightly ridiculous, Superintendent . . .'

'*Chief* Superintendent.'

'Chief Superintendent Whatever-your-name-is . . .'

'Tallboy.'

'*Chief* Superintendent Tallboy. A woman's been murdered. I hardly knew her. I certainly didn't like her. I can add nothing to what I've already told . . .'

'That you've seen her in the garden?'

'Only once. Twice at the most.'

'The back garden?'

'I've already . . .'

'*The back garden*?'

'Yes.' Philippa Holmes sighed dramatically. 'I've seen the woman in her back garden. Once. Possibly twice. Now, I've already told . . .'

'From your bedroom window.'

'From my bedroom window.' She spoke each word deliberately; she allowed a slight pause between each word, as if she was talking to an idiot child.

'You looked,' said Tallboy flatly.

'What?'

'You looked. You watched.'

'That's an outrageous . . .'

'You saw what she was doing. You didn't merely catch sight of her from the corner of your eye . . . it wasn't like *that*. You were interested enough to note what she was doing.'

'All right.' The eyebrows had lowered. The eyes blazed dangerously. 'Let's assume . . .'

'Let's *accept*.'

'. . . that for a moment my curiosity got the better of me and I . . .'

'On her hands and knees, digging something up with her hands.'

'Yes,' she snapped.

'Where?'

'What?'

'Where?'

'I've already . . .'

'Precisely?'

'Towards the bottom of the garden.'

'From your bedroom window you could point out the exact position.'

'I could . . . if I so desired.'

'Will you?'

'No. I'm damned . . .'

'Madam.' For the first time Tallboy smiled. It was a quick, tight smile. Without humour. Without friendliness. He said, 'You own a Mini. Your own car. Not your husband's.' In a slow, sing-song tone he gave the colour and registration number of the car. He said, 'I've told you who I am — *what* I am — not in order to impress, but in order to remove any doubts from your mind. I can, if I so desire, send out a divisional instruction. To every police officer under my supervision. Tightening up road traffic regulations. Especially where a Mini is concerned. One specific Mini. It may well be that you never drive above the legal speed limit. That your brakes and tyres can't be faulted. That you always obey traffic signs. That you always carry your driving licence and certificate of insurance around with you. That you're the one person in the world who *never* breaks the road traffic law.'

'Are you threatening me?' she gasped.

Tallboy turned and looked a question at Stone.

'No, sir.' Stone shook his head in mock wonderment. 'I haven't heard anybody being threatened . . . only good advice.'

'From the bedroom window,' said Tallboy gently. 'You could point out exactly where you saw Annie Miller.'

'Very well.' The words seemed to almost choke her. 'Come this way.'

'No.' Tallboy shook his head. 'Constable Stone.'

'Could I . . .' Her nostrils quivered. 'Could I call you a bastard?'

'Not by birth,' said Tallboy calmly. 'By inclination, if you wish. That would be no more than opinion . . . *your* opinion.'

She stared hatred at him for a moment, then turned.

Tallboy said, 'Go with Mrs Holmes, constable. She's anxious to do all she can to further the enquiry.'

Rowe telephoned his news to the Incident Centre. He'd traced the fuel merchant who supplied Annie Miller with coal. A Sopworth merchant. The coal was delivered and the note pushed through the letter box. Payment was made by post . . . always. A postal order, sent in an envelope with a Bordfield postmark. The delivery? A regular delivery, two sacks once a fortnight. No, it was a small, two-man business, himself and his son . . . neither of them had ever seen Annie Miller.

The man at the Incident Centre said, 'Another dead-end, sir.'

'One gets the feeling,' murmured Rowe.

'Sir?'

'That in some spooky way she didn't even want to *exist*.'

Mevagissey. Once upon a time it was a schooner port and, as the hillside plummets down to the quay-line, the individual houses seem to cling like frightened children to the steep slope. It is pure Cornwall; magnificent, despite its miniaturisation; rugged, uncompromising and (or so it seems) tanned and seamed by the weather and sea which has battered its face for centuries. It is still a fishing port and, when the narrow, twisting streets are milled with holiday-makers the men of the sea make a passable living hiring out their boats to 'townies' anxious to flex their muscles hunting the sharks which still prowl in the deeps off Black Head and beyond St Austell Bay.

On this day, Tuesday October 21st, the two killers sat in their car, parked on the most popular of the official car parks, out alongside the outer harbour and within sight and spray-distance of the sea which crashed and ran along the first breakwater. A steady force eight carried the white-tops in at an angle and the mist from the shattered water gave lips the taste of salt; the broken fury of frustrated waves hissed at it; soaked the surface of the narrow car park and dried white and sparkling against the bodywork of the vehicle.

'It's cold,' complained the younger man.

The elder man remained silent and peered through the spray-soaked windscreen.

'Will he know where we are?'

'He'll find us.' The elder man turned the ignition key, the engine throbbed gently at an idling speed, and the elder man flicked the wiper switch to clear the windscreen. He stopped the wiper, stopped the engine, then added, 'No excuses. We botched it.'

'She made us botch it.'

'No excuses,' repeated the elder man. 'The excuses ended . . . before you were born.'

THIRTEEN

They were like animals strapped to vivisection tables. Rows of them, unable to move, unable to help themselves or each other. Women. Jewesses . . . or if not Jewesses in the pure sense, women with the 'taint' of Jewish blood in their veins. Jewesses from Poland, from Russia, from Czechoslovakia, from Hungary. Even from the Fatherland itself. Women, because their opposite sex could at least be made to work themselves to the point of death before being exterminated; because the 'work-life' of a starving man was considered to be slightly longer than the 'work-life' of a starving woman.

'And,' Gebhart explained, 'there may be some truth in the belief that the female is able to tolerate pain better – longer – than the male.'

Gebhardt strolled down the lines of tables. He paused at each table, ignored the frozen terror on the woman's face, then deliberately — almost off-handedly — sliced into living flesh with the scalpel. He tried to re-create the horrific wounds of the battle-field. A leg opened to the bone, here. A stomach wound squirting life-blood, there. Limbs, bodies, heads, faces . . . like some mad artist slashing brush-strokes of scarlet as he passed, he led his tiny entourage around a charnel-house of his own making.

If he heard the screams — the wild curses in half a dozen different languages — he ignored them. The agony — the keels of torture — were part of the experiment. Wounded men screamed. Wounded men felt the incandescent pain. Wounded men had not had pain-killing drugs.

'An experiment must be as near to perfection as possible,' he explained. 'Our soldiers are brought home to be repaired, therefore, we must *know* things. We must be ready to fight the infection. We must be prepared.'

Therefore, his underlings rubbed shavings, broken glass, mud, excreta into the wounds. The filth of war was deliberately introduced into the wounds, in an attempt to create gangrene. Then, when the victim was on the point of death, drugs were tried. Varying doses. Varying drugs. Varying mixtures.

'If we can stop the foul flesh of these creatures from festering, we can be assured that the good flesh of the fighting men will respond. If we can't, we must try again. Try harder.'

And Helena and Irma believed him. They *all* believed him. And why should they *not* believe him? He was professor Karl Gebhardt and what he was doing had the blessing of Heinrich Himmler.

It was a triumph. Not the triumph Gebhardt sought, but a triumph, nevertheless. The propaganda — the systematic and never-ending brain-washing of a whole generation — ensured that young women like Helena and Irma saw nothing evil in what was happening. It was necessary. Part of the great war effort. It was a form of patriotism, and it would have been a treachery to have drawn back.

In August 1942 both Helena and Irma were promoted to trainee wardresses at Ravensbrück.

FOURTEEN

'There.' Tallboy pointed.

The rain came down in a steady stream of liquid misery. The four men detailed for the task of digging up the water-logged earth cursed themselves for being unfortunate enough to be sheltering in the Incident Centre when Tallboy had marched in. 'Four volunteers. You, you, you and you. You'll need spades.' And now, despite macs and wellington boots, they were soaking wet . . . as, indeed, was Tallboy. The long harsh grass and weeds from the neglected garden had saturated their trousers at about knee-height. The rainwater ran in streams from their shapeless hats.

'How far down?' One of the men grunted the question as he stood, spade poised, and glowered his digust at Tallboy.

'Not too deep,' Tallboy said. 'And don't go at it as if you're cutting the first sod for the Channel Tunnel.'

'Scrape it away?' The questioner was one of the old hands at the game. He was no less wet – no less uncomfortable – than the rest, but he'd been on this caper before. It was part of the job and, despite the flash adverts, it wasn't the cleanest and most comfortable job in creation. He said, 'If there's summat there, and *she* only used her hands . . .'

'Scrape it away,' agreed Tallboy.

The man ready to hurl the blade of the spade into the ground sighed and lowered his spade.

It was a patch of earth; about a square yard of soil in which few weeds had found root. It was near the bole of an ancient ash, at the bottom of the rear garden. Of the whole garden – front and rear – it was the one tiny piece which looked as if it *might* have been cultivated.

They scraped. Less than six inches down they found what they were looking for. It was a beautifully constructed box, about nine inches by six inches, and about four inches deep. It was wrapped in oilskin, and one of the men bent, lifted it carefully from the soil and handed it to Tallboy. Tallboy took it to the path, unfolded the oilskin then, with some difficulty because of its perfect fit, lifted the lid.

The expression 'A King's Ransom'. It was there; the box was more than half-filled with gems and jewellery the like of which Tallboy had never before seen. Rings and brooches, necklaces and pendants. Nor were they paste; there was about them the sparkle and life which even the best of fake jewellery can never imitate. Most of the gems were diamonds, many in settings of worked gold. There was a brooch in the shape of the Star of David; one triangle in diamonds, the other triangle in rubies; one single piece which, in itself, was worth a small fortune. There was a necklace of matching pearls; rings with tiny diamonds clustered around a single centre stone; ear-rings which shimmered and splashed rainbow-coloured lights back at the gaping officers. It was all there; wealth almost beyond belief, lying in the box which had been buried just below the surface of the soil.

'That's it,' breathed Tallboy. 'The 'Top-up Fund'. My God! She could have lived like a princess.'

He was a fat man, swarthy, stocky and with a pate completely bald except for a fringe of snow-white hair which linked his ears behind his skull; a skull which seemed a size too large for his body, even a size too large for his face. He carried the stamp of his race with a pride which was almost an arrogance. Fanaticism made his dark eyes shine as if a bulb illuminated their impatient gaze. He had a name. Within his own kind he was respected almost to the point of worship. He had a name, but he was known as The Hunter.

'Look,' argued the younger of the killers, 'it's only newspaper headlines. We did it right . . . *they've* got it wrong.'

'*Jewish Woman Slain.*' The Hunter read the words, then paused. The impression was that he was about to spit in outraged disgust. He said, 'You would know about newspapers? You would know about what newspapers can do? I tell you. They print lies and people believe. There — in the newspaper, on the radio — they believe. A mistake, you say? So . . . a mistake? Do the animals who still believe think it is a mistake?'

'Does it matter?' The younger man fought back weakly.

'It matters!' snapped The Hunter. 'You are young. You are foolish. Let me tell you . . . newspapers can destroy a nation's will to live. I *know*. The camps. The gas chambers. Why should a whole people walk quietly to its own destruction? *Why*? Because that was all we were fit for. Vermin to be destroyed. We believed, because we'd been told. Every day. Newspapers. Radio. The media. We were Jews — we were the 'Christ-killers' — the camps and the ovens were all we were fit for. *And we believed!* Our dignity was torn from us. Our right to live was denied. A whole nation made to feel unclean, convinced that to fight would only add to our foulness.'

'This is England,' protested the younger man.

'Sure — this is England, that was Germany.' The eyes flashed and the words slashed like naked blades. 'You think this place is safe. You think it can't happen here. Lemme tell you — it can happen *anywhere*. That headline. It's been read already. By scum. By animals. They don't wear jackboots. And why? Because they haven't yet been *issued* with jackboots. That's all. That's the only reason. But they're thinking. It can be done. One more Jew can be strung up on wire. One, why not more? Why not let *us* hang a few more? They're around. They still march. They get braver. Now they *call* themselves what they are. So? This is England?'

'I'm — I'm sorry.'

'Peace.' The voice quietened a little. 'You don't know, my son. You didn't live through it. Peace, eh?'

'Peace,' murmured the younger man.

The elder killer spoke and asked, 'How do we counter it?'

'You have to ask?' The Hunter's voice was sad.

'I know.' The elder killer sighed. 'Not for publicity . . . as a warning.' He paused, then added, 'But no need for both of us.'

'Look . . .' began the younger killer.

'Learn to take orders,' said the elder killer sadly. 'Learn to obey.'

'Not you,' said The Hunter, and his voice carried absolute authority. 'There is need for dignity. I want no outbursts. The pride of age is all we need.' Then in a gentler voice, to the elder man, 'It is necessary.'

'Of course.'

'You understand?'

The elder man nodded, then asked, 'We fight?'

It was a question; a curiosity with overtones of wry humour.

The hunter said, 'We fight, my old friend. Today we *always* fight.'

They stared at it, open-eyed and open-mouthed. In the box — out in the weather, on the garden path — it had seemed almost unbelievable. Here, set out on one of the tables, it seemed even more unbelievable. Like something from an *Arabian Nights* fantasy. Wealth beyond dreams. Craftsmanship in precious metal and gem stones, the like of which none of them had seen before.

Blayde growled, 'One thing for sure. It's not nicked. Any one of those pieces would have been photographed and circulated to every force in the country.'

'It can't have been *hers*,' argued Tallboy. 'Hell's teeth . . . nobody lives in poverty while owning that lot.'

'It's not nicked,' insisted Blayde.

Kelly said, 'I'm inclined to agree. Some of those brooches, some of those pendants . . . millionaire baubles. They *must* have been circulated.'

'It doesn't click,' muttered Tallboy.

'Nothing in this bloody case clicks.' Blayde's frustration boiled over. 'She lived in a dump, she could have lived at the Savoy. With that lot she could have had half the crappy nobility of central Europe fawning on her, but she wouldn't even join the W.I. She didn't struggle. Christ, she could have paid for the Brigade of Guards to do sentry duty on her front doorstep. She could . . .'

'She sold some of it,' interrupted Tallboy.

'Sold it!' Blayde glared. 'If what's gone is anything *like* that lot, she didn't sell it. She gave the bloody stuff away.'

'Who?' Stone asked the question. He couldn't drag his eyes away from the fortune set out on the table.

'Aye, who?' grunted Blayde.

Kelly said, 'I know the fences. I think I know most of 'em. They wouldn't touch that stuff. It's way out of their league.'

'If the price was right,' argued Tallboy.

'If she was *giving* it away,' agreed Blayde.

'And,' said Tallboy, 'only the first piece. After that, he'd trust her.'

'Right.' Blayde straightened up from the table. He spoke to the group around him and, from his tone, it was clear he'd reached a firm decision. 'For the time being, forget the murder. Spend today tying up loose ends. From tomorrow we approach it from another angle. Lock up the house. A uniformed copper on guard, day and night, to keep the vandals and rubbernecks away. Everybody else . . . I want to know the buyer. Receivers, jewellers, gold merchants, collectors. Everybody. Here at Bordfield, at Lessford, anywhere up North. And make it clear it isn't 'knock'. It's legitimate stuff, and there's no reason why they *shouldn't* have bought it . . . whatever 'it' was. But I want to know who knew her well enough to buy. And where she *said* it came from. I want to know who the hell she was, and why the hell we come up against a contradiction, whichever way we turn.' He paused, then concluded, 'And now the media. Nothing! For the moment, we keep this thing up our sleeve. Check it through with me, Mr Tallboy. Sergeant Kelly, you be witness. List it and I'll give you a receipt, then it goes into the bank vault of a friend of mine.'

INTERVIEW

ONE

In retrospect, I can truthfully say that I was neither swayed nor tempted by the offer of a quite magnificent fee; in the event I refused more than my normal charge for myself and my junior. Nor (and here I may be on slightly less firm ground) had my acceptance anything to do with my high regard for Armstrong. Reginald Armstrong was a young, able and very enthusiastic solicitor, and we'd met some two years previously as a result of a case in which I'd represented his client.* It was not a case of which I was over-proud, despite the fact that I'd cleared his client of a murder charge but, as a result of that case and the friendship which had grown up between us since our meeting, we'd kept in touch. Letters mostly; gossip and harmless tittle-tattle, as between uncle and nephew. And, on one occasion, I'd been able to offer the hospitality of my flat when Armstrong and his charming wife, Ruth, had visited London for a short summer break.

Nevertheless, I was surprised when Armstrong telephoned me one evening. (Consulting my diary, I note that it was on the evening of Sunday, October the 26th.) He sounded agitated; one might almost say excited. This was not unusual. To a staid old barrister like myself, the Armstrongs of this world give the impression of being in a perpetual state of near-panic. He said he was at King's Cross, that he'd just trained down from the North, and would it be convenient for him to call at my flat immediately. I know I smiled my forbearance, agreed without hesitation then, when I'd replaced the receiver, had felt guilty at the twinge of annoyance as I'd closed Prittie's most interesting biography of Willy Brandt.

It took him less than thirty minutes to arrive and, as I heard the cab stop in the street, I opened the door to greet him.

He looked as healthy and as young as ever. And as eager. In all my long years in the forensic world I have known nobody as ready

---

Man of Law by John Wainwright, Macmillan, 1980.

to take up a lost cause; nobody as anxious to grasp the stinging-nettle of law and rip its roots from ancient and, perhaps, sour earth. Therefore, I might have known. I might, at least, have guessed; Reginald without Ruth; the suitcase in one hand, but the briefcase in the other.

He paid off the cab driver, tucked the briefcase under the arm with which he was holding the suitcase, and we shook hands.

'It's good to see you, sir,' he grinned. 'Worth the journey just to see your face.'

'The feeling's mutual,' I assured him. 'We ancient legal eagles don't do much entertaining, more's the pity.'

I fussed around him a little, as he hung his overcoat and hat in the hall. He left his suitcase in the hall, too, but I still remained sublimely stupid even when he carried the briefcase with him when we moved into the living room and settled in front of the fire.

'Whisky?' I suggested.

'Well watered, please.'

'You'll be staying the night?' I poured whisky, then added water and ice cubes.

'I was hoping you'd extend an invitation,' he smiled.

'But of course.' I carried the glasses across the room. 'Mrs Leach, my cleaning lady, keeps the spare bedroom ready. She diligently airs the sheets. I think she pops the electric blanket on, while she vacs and polishes around.'

We sat and chatted for about ten minutes; exchanging news and bringing each other up to date with our respective lives. Then he suddenly looked solemn, leaned forward in his armchair, unsnapped the fasteners on his briefcase and made the first move in what was to prove one of the few truly interesting episodes of my somewhat dull life.

He said, 'I — er — I'm trespassing on our friendship, sir.'

'Really?' I chuckled. 'One of the many reasons for having friends ... surely?'

'I should have approached your clerk. Made an appointment to see you in chambers.'

'It's more comfortable here,' I assured him.

'It's this.' He handed me two typed foolscap sheets, stapled together at one corner. 'That's a short synopsis. I've taken the case . . . because it's both interesting and unusual. I'd like you and Smith-Hopkinson to plead.'

'The old team,' I murmured.

He remained silent while I read. He watched my face. I have no doubt he saw the periodic looks of surprise and, perhaps, distaste. But being Armstrong, he refrained from making comment until I'd finished reading, gone back to re-read certain passages, then handed the sheets back to him.

'You've seen the man?' I asked.

'Not yet. I've arranged to deliver him to the police on Wednesday.'

'The police know this?'

'No . . . not yet.'

'You're on shaky ground,' I sighed. 'If you know the identity of the murderer and being an officer of the court — which by reason of your status as solicitor you are — '

'Not 'murderer',' he said quietly.

'He killed her.' I stared. 'That means he's the . . .'

'He killed her,' he agreed.

'In a particularly foul manner.'

He nodded.

'Deliberately,' I emphasised.

'Quite deliberately,' he agreed.

'Certainly with the required malice aforethought.'

'He visited her in order to kill her.' He nodded.

'In that case, there seems little doubt — *no* doubt, that I can see — but that he committed . . .'

'There's a plea, sir.' His interruption was intense. So much so that I thought I detected a slight tremor in his voice. 'A defence. A complete defence. I've checked and re-checked. This man who calls himself 'The Hunter'. He assures me he can find the witnesses. Enough evidence. He can provide it — *will* provide it — in time for the Crown Court hearing.'

'Who is he?' I asked bluntly. '*What* is he? I tend to be highly suspicious of people who hide their identity behind these ridiculous titles.'

He told me, then continued, 'There are men, sir. Dedicated men.

A mere handful, each in charge of his own small organisation. They work independently, but keep in close touch. Their strength — the only strength they have — is their anonymity.'

'If he can be relied upon . . .' I said slowly.

'He can. One hundred per cent.'

'And you claim there's a defence?'

'Yes, sir.' He closed his briefcase, placed it on the carpet alongside his chair, leaned forward and, in effect, pleaded his cause.

It was, of course, outrageous. Had any man, other than Armstrong, even suggested such a line of defence I might have brought the conversation to an abrupt conclusion prior to turning him from the flat. But this was my friend. A good friend. More than that even, a good solicitor. Therefore, I listened, I argued, I was met by counter-argument, I was tempted and I fell.

I suppose the truth is that all barristers are frustrated actors. We have a yen to be dramatic . . . even melodramatic. Few of us ever are, of course. We trot along to the various courts, stand up, say our set pieces, harry some miserable witness under cross-examination, then sit back knowing full well what the verdict will be. My life in a nutshell. I took silk because I deluded myself that stuff gowns rarely attract the *cause célèbre* . . . I soon discovered that silk gowns suffered the same disadvantage, for the simple reason that the *cause célèbre* was a most unusual happening. I concentrated upon Criminal Law because (in my innocence) I visualised myself as the Great Defender, saving the wrongly accused man from the noose. The sad fact is that capital punishment was abolished before I became even moderately successful and, as I found to my cost, wrongly accused murderers were at a distinct premium and almost *all* murderers were pathetic creatures quite incapable of managing even a very humdrum existence. In the event I ended up pleading for snivelling wretches, charged with theft in its various guises, with the accused noticeably more contrite at the fact that he'd been caught than at the fact that he'd committed a criminal act.

Thus are dreams shattered and, over the years, heeled into the mud of reality.

But this was it. The *cause célèbre* I'd always yearned for. And if I failed, what matter? I was unmarried. To the best of my knowledge,

I had no children. I was settled — one might almost say rooted — in my life of bachelorhood, but already I was toying with the possibility of retirement. Unlike the Bench, the Bar is ever justling with young bloods anxious to make a name for themselves, and I was wearying of this never-ending fight to keep ahead. I was tired of listening to the same old stories of court room squabbles which, in the telling, moved farther and farther from the unvarnished and quite unexciting truth. I had an adequate nest-egg safely invested; enough to keep me in comparative comfort for the rest of my days. I could, if I wished, earn myself a little extra pin-money by droning forensic platitudes at bored listeners at a university here and there. Given the urge, I might even write one more textbook devoted to (say) Common Law, or Constitutional Law, or even Jurisprudence . . . a boring but monumentally safe subject in that no lawyer specialising in Chancery Law is ever able to make two and two come to a simple and straightforward four without the aid of a law library and, even then, his answer will be hedged in with enough qualifications to enable him to say 'I told you so', should his listener or reader mistake the four for five.

Criminal Law, on the other hand . . .

But I digress. Suffice to say that by midnight and after some few more drinks and cigarettes, I agreed to accept the brief. Admittedly, I felt a little like a man who, having jumped from the cliff tops at Beachy Head, was flapping his arms in the hope that he might fly, but no matter. I had faith in Armstrong and if I failed it wouldn't be my first failure. Whereas, if I won . . .

'Smith-Hopkinson?' asked Armstrong.

'I'll ask him,' I promised.

'I've kept check. I even looked it up, before I set off for here. He hasn't yet taken silk.'

'He's toying with the idea.' I smiled. 'At a guess he's deliberating . . . whether the title of Queen's Counsel will attract eligible young ladies or frighten them off.'

'He deserves it,' observed Armstrong.

'It's his for the asking,' I agreed. Then I said, 'Tomorrow morning — at about ten — you must come to the chambers and make formal request from the clerk. Otherwise . . .'

'And if he refuses?' Armstrong suddenly looked worried. 'If he gives the brief to another member of the chambers?'

'My boy.' I chuckled with glee at this young man's innocence. 'It's the *look* of the thing that matters. Technically, he *could* refuse — technically he could give the brief to some other member of the chambers — but I'll have a private word with him and emphasise what he may and may not do. They only *think* they run the various chambers, you know. They read of their importance in various books . . . none of which are written by practising barristers.'

TWO

In fact *I* delivered Gold to the police. It seemed best; indeed, it seemed best that I make the acquaintance of my client as soon as possible. I therefore journeyed north on Tuesday, October 28th, booked in at a good hotel and, with the connivance of Armstrong, met Samuel Gold in my hotel bedroom that evening. He was an older man than I had expected; at a guess he was about my own age. I say 'at a guess' because I suspect he lopped a few years from his true age . . . for reasons best known to himself.

Nevertheless, I liked him. I questioned him. Hard. His answers were both direct and simple. No evasions. No excuses. He had (to use his own expression) 'executed' her; delayed justice for her past infamies.

Armstrong was with me, and I could see the puzzled expression on his face.

I said, 'I have only newspaper reports. The suggestion is that she didn't struggle.'

'No struggle,' said Gold.

'You don't find that strange?'

'As they grow older, they develop consciences.' He smiled sadly. 'They have to live with themselves. That might not be easy.'

'There's death . . . and death,' murmured Armstrong.

Gold nodded. It was apparent that, in agreeing with Armstrong, he was not necessarily following Armstrong's line of thought.

'We plead 'Not Guilty',' I reminded him.

'I'm in your hands.'

'That,' I mused, 'calls for some carefully thought-out strategy. To give yourself up, admitting that you killed the woman . . . then to plead 'Not Guilty'. You'll be asked questions.'

'I realise that.'

'Don't answer them,' said Armstrong. 'Don't say a word without the okay from either Mr Whitehouse or myself. Whether we're present or not.'

'I don't mind going to prison.' There was simple dignity in the remark.

'*I* mind.' I put on a show of impatience. 'Armstrong minds. My junior, Smith-Hopkinson, minds. This is not a show trial.'

THREE

But, of course, it was a 'show trial'.

When the time arrived Lessford Crown Court would, temporarily, become the focus point of every national in the land. And of reporters from other lands. How could it be otherwise? The stench from those ovens had not yet dissipated. The cries of those human skeletons had not yet died away. It would take a generation, and probably another generation, before the attempted genocide of the Jewish nation could be viewed objectively.

I was of an age group, and we'd seen for ourselves. To us, it wasn't some second-hand horror story. We *knew*. And we knew other things, too. For example that men and women of our own age, once Germany was on the brink of defeat — once the camps and the gassing-sheds had been opened up — had denied all association with the Nazi regime. Indeed, in the mid-forties it had been a rather sick joke. Where had all the Nazis gone? Where *were* all those people who'd raised Hitler to the position of dictator?

Having stood by and allowed an abomination, they had perpetrated a national lie ... that they hadn't *really* wanted Hitler as their leader. That a mere handful of men had marched behind the crooked cross and that the rest had simply gone along because everybody else was going along.

And today?

Today there was national guilt. Communal guilt. The new Germany had taken the pendulum and swung it, if anything, too far the other way. Men and women were accepting a guilt which wasn't theirs; they were bowing their heads in a shame of which they were not a part.

God, it was certainly going to be a show trial.

And as I lay in the gloom of my hotel bedroom I forced myself to perform certain heart searchings. My beloved *cause célèbre*. It was already under way and, short of backing out of the case, there wasn't a thing I could do to stop it. But now I had it, did I want it? Did I want the world's press – the world's media – to hang onto my every word? Was I prepared to risk what little reputation I had in one last desperate throw? In short ... ambition. That had become the name of the game.

Was I ambitious?

The truth was I wasn't sure. Like every other youngster who accepts the Bar as a chosen profession, I'd had visions of being a second Marshall Hall when I'd tried my first wig for size; I'd already decided upon the Criminal Law, I'd already decided that 'pleading' was to be my chosen field and, in those days, the legendary 'Great Pleader' hadn't seemed *so* wonderful. But that had been youthful ambition based upon crass ignorance. The years had brought wisdom. I was still a 'pleader' – I'd be a 'pleader' to the end of my days – but the unhappy truth was that the greater the scoundrel the easier it was to earn the title of 'mouthpiece' or even 'shyster', and that was a tag I had no wish to burden myself with. I was old-fashioned enough to value honour and self-respect. I was self-opinionated enough to believe that my fellows respected me and, if they did, I had no desire to lose any of that respect. I was guilty of one of the seven deadly sins ... pride.

Great cases make great barristers. But, equally, great cases destroy run-of-the-mill barristers, and I had yet to convince myself that I was not, in the final analysis, merely run-of-the-mill. Fortunate in that I had not yet been found out. *Very* fortunate that my dreamed of *cause célèbre* had so far eluded me.

I slept little that night. I spent much of the darkness trying to come to terms with my own slightly creaking ideas of what was right and what was wrong; of what I wanted and what I did not want. I rose early, showered, dressed then went for a brisk walk along the pavements of Lessford before I returned to the hotel for breakfast . . . and I *still* wasn't sure.

FOUR

An old barrister's trick. Split-second punctuality. I needed every ruse in the book and, having telephoned the police and arranged a meeting in order to deliver the man responsible for Annie Miller's death, I kept that appointment . . . precisely. I knew they'd be waiting; it isn't often a Q.C. telephones to detect a major crime by accompanying the man the police are hunting into the Incident Centre at the heart of the crime. Human nature being what it is, the police representative would be there an hour (perhaps more) before the agreed time. And, whatever their rank, even senior police officers are human. They (assuming there was more than one) would have been watching the clock, checking their watches; waiting and, as they waited, becoming less and less sure of themselves.

The trick, therefore. Not to be late, but to convince them that you're *going* to be late. It gives you that first, all-important edge.

The man who met me as I walked through the door of the village hall was a certain Detective Chief Superintendent Blayde. The name was appropriate. The expression 'sharp' sprang to mind immediately. Not sharp in the wide-boy sense, but meaning a man with whom it might be unwise to take too many liberties. In the past I'd had the unenviable task of cross-examining such men in the witness box and with them the hope of intimidation was quite forlorn. They cannot be shaken. They possess an arrogance which refuses to admit even the possibility of mistake.

We shook hands, having introduced ourselves, and his grip was firm, cool and dry. No sweating palms with this one. No limp-fish empty politeness. It was a little like touching blades (no pun intended) prior to a duel.

And yet he'd been on his feet, waiting. Pacing his impatience, perhaps. I hoped so. At least that made him human enough to be vulnerable to the right tactics.

He introduced me to what I took to be his second-in-command. A Chief Superintendent Tallboy. Younger, perhaps, than Blayde and, because the word 'detective' wasn't included in the introduction a man I guessed to be a uniformed officer when major crime wasn't being handled.

Other than the three of us, the Incident Centre was empty. I think the surprise showed in my face as I looked round.

'Just the three of us,' said Blayde. 'I thought it best.' Then he frowned and added, 'I thought it would be the *four* of us.'

'He'll be along,' I promised.

'The man who murdered Annie Miller?'

'The man responsible for her death,' I answered carefully.

Blayde waved a hand, and we sat in a group at one end of a trestle-table. Tallboy produced cigarettes, Blayde produced a lighter and moved a cheap ashtray to within easy reach. Like chess players, we each waited for the other to make the first move. We smoked cigarettes and watched each other's faces.

Tallboy cleared his throat, and said, 'He could be a nutter, sir.'

I smiled and tapped ash into the ash-tray.

Blayde rumbled, 'It *has* been known.'

'Not this time,' I assured them.

Blayde, having broken his silence, said, 'No deals . . . if that's what you're waiting for.'

'Bail.' I spoke for the first time since we'd sat down.

'That's not up to us.' Blayde took over as spokesman.

I smiled and said, 'I apply, you oppose . . . I don't get it.'

'It's not always like that.'

'Enough times to make it usual.'

Blayde gave the matter some thought, then said, 'Okay — we don't oppose bail — what do *we* get?'

'The man responsible for the death of Annie Miller.'

'The murderer?'

'An expression I won't use,' I said mildly.

'Eh?'

'The plea will be 'Not Guilty'.'

'In that case . . .'

'You'll *charge* him with the crime,' I interrupted. 'And if you don't charge him, you'll charge nobody . . . take my word for that. But he isn't a murderer — and he won't *be* a murderer — unless a jury labels him as such.'

'You're here to play ducks and drakes.' Blayde's eyes narrowed.

'I'm here to protect the interests of my client.' I, too, could put steel in my voice. 'He'll answer reasonable questions. He'll answer *nothing* unless either I or his solicitor advise him otherwise.'

'Mr Whitehouse.' Tallboy's voice was reasonable, without being either pleading or subservient. 'In this division we don't play the game of 'verbals'. If your client doesn't say anything outside the presence of his lawyer, nothing will be invented. But if he *does* . . . rest assured, he'll have said it.'

I nodded. I *was* reassured. Instinctively I liked this officer; there was a nice mix of ruthlessness tempered by humanity in the man. And if the Bar teaches nothing else, it teaches instinct; the ability to size up a man (and some women) within minutes of a first meeting.

As for the other one, Blayde. A hard nut. Not bent; above all else, not bent. But without mercy. I tried to appraise him, without him being aware of it, and I came to some firm conclusions. That the world was fortunate that he was a policeman. As a villain, he would have been equally merciless. The expression, 'It takes a bastard to beat a bastard' applied wholeheartedly to this one. I thought he was the most complete . . .

'Have you weighed me up yet?'

The blunt question caught me off balance. Completely off balance. There I'd been, assessing the man while, at the same time giving the impression that I was *not* assessing him . . . and he'd known! It seemed little short of mind reading.

I felt my face colour, but managed to keep my voice steady, as I said, 'A brutal man, but that includes brutal honesty. I think you'd have your tongue torn out rather than lie.'

He growled, 'Don't bet money on it,' but I thought I saw the faint sheen of something not too far removed from pleasure at the back of his eyes.

We nodded, gently, at each other, as if acknowledging mutual respect, then I said, 'Right. Can we get down to details?'

'You've promised to produce the man we want,' said Blayde.

'Yes.' I glanced at my wrist watch. 'He'll be here in four minutes exactly.'

'A rare one for punctuality . . . *if* he turns up.'

'He'll turn up. With his solicitor.'

'Well protected?' There was a hint of a sneer in Blayde's questioning remark.

'Two for, two against . . . that's not unfair,' I countered.

'This isn't a game.'

'Nor to us,' I agreed. 'But there are rules, nevertheless.'

'Are we allowed to ask him questions?' asked Tallboy.

'Certainly . . . within limits.'

'And if we aren't satisfied?' demanded Blayde.

'Satisfied?'

'That he *is* the murderer?'

'You're using that word again, superintendent,' I chided him. 'But — and here you have my solemn word — if you charge anybody other than my client you'll be charging an innocent man.'

'Meaning he *is* the murderer?'

'Not quite, Mr Blayde. Meaning that *if* Annie Miller was murdered, my client was responsible.'

'She was murdered all right.'

'An opinion.' I smiled. 'You're entitled to hold it. You're not yet entitled to treat it as a proven fact.'

Tallboy said, 'You mentioned something about 'details'.'

'An Occasional Court. Tomorrow morning,' I said.

'It might be arranged,' said Blayde.

Tallboy added, 'Let's say it *can* be arranged?'

'No opposition to bail?'

'No opposition.' Blayde breathed deeply.

'And when you've asked him all the questions you wish to ask him today?'

'You're not asking *us* to bail him?' Blayde glared.

'To the Occasional Court.'

'Be damned for a tale. If he's the . . .'

'You've already agreed not to oppose bail, superintendent.'

'That's not the same . . .'

'What had you in mind for those twenty-four hours?' I asked pointedly.

'Which twenty-four hours?'

'While he's in police custody? Before the Occasional Court?'

'He'll be in a police cell. Where else?'

'While you're making enquiries? Checking his story?'

Blayde nodded.

'Mr Blayde. Mr Tallboy.' I stubbed out my cigarette into the ash-tray. I handed my own cigarettes round and, as we lighted the new cigarettes from Tallboy's lighter, I said, 'A possible solution. Ask the questions. As many questions as you wish, in order to verify the authenticity of my client's admission. Check his answers. Then — tomorrow morning before the Occasional Court — charge him. And if you don't oppose bail . . .'

'Ducks and drakes,' growled Blayde.

Tallboy said, 'What guarantees have we? That he won't skip?'

'My guarantee. His solicitor's guarantee. And behind us The Bar Council and The Law Society.'

Blayde said, 'You sound bloody sure.'

'I *am* sure.'

'We'll see.' The half-promise didn't come easy. 'Let's have a session with him . . . then we'll see.'

I was satisfied. I'd won what I wanted; perhaps more than I'd expected. I knew Armstrong would be delighted. I hoped Gold would be appreciative. As for the man who insisted upon being called 'The Hunter' . . . frankly he was a fanatic and I'd long passed the time in life when fanatics were more than mild irritants.

FIVE

The seating arrangement had changed. We still sat at the same trestle-table, but this time the trestle-table was a sort of No Man's Land. Gold sat on one side, flanked on the right by myself and on the left by Armstrong. Opposite Gold sat Blayde and on Blayde's left sat Tallboy. Both Tallboy and Armstrong were making copious notes on foolscap. Blayde's eyes never left the face of Gold and, in fairness, Gold never once dropped his gaze from Blayde's hard stare.

Cigarettes were still being smoked and the atmosphere, though tense, was nevertheless civilised. When he'd first entered the Incident Centre Gold had even shaken hands with both Blayde and Tallboy. Nor had those two officers denied him this tiny gesture of politeness. Then the questioning had started.

Name, address, age and occupation. Gold had given his address as 'Of No Fixed Abode', then modified this by adding, 'At the present moment — until further notice — I'm staying at the Bordfield Railway Hotel.' He'd described his occupation as General Dealer and, when pressed to be more specific, he'd added, 'Antiques. Objets d'art.'

'You buy and sell?' suggested Blayde.

'I do.' Gold nodded.

'A good living?' asked Blayde politely.

'Moderately good.'

I smiled to myself. This Blayde was a sly dog. He was approaching the subject very deviously. His object (quite a legitimate object, from his point of view) was to get Gold relaxed and at ease; to give this life-and-death inquisition the external trappings of a friendly conversation between men of differing interests. It was a technique, and not an easy technique, but sometimes a very *successful* technique.

Blayde said, 'That was why you were here in Rimstone . . . presumably.'

'What?'

'To collect antiques. Things you might buy and sell.'

'No.'

'Really?' I kept a straight face, but inside I congratulated Blayde upon the genuine look of mild surprise which accompanied the question.

Gold said, 'I thought Mr Whitehouse had . . .'

'Just the two of us for the moment, Mr Gold.' Blayde moved a friendly hand. 'Basics. You know Rimstone?'

'Yes.' Gold nodded.

'Well?'

'Fairly well.'

'How many times have you visited the village?'

'Twice. No . . . three times. This visit is my fourth.'

'Good.' Blayde smiled. 'Let's be accurate.'

Gold waited. I could sense his growing tenseness. Very gradually Blayde was approaching the questions which would demand very careful answers. Tallboy and Armstrong continued to record the question and answer session.

Blayde murmured, 'The reason for your first visit?'

'To — er — to find the village. I'd never been here before.'

'By car?'

'Yes, by car.'

'Alone?'

'Yes, alone.'

'Did you find it easily?'

'I — er — I followed the map. And the signposts. I found it easily.'

'Did you stay in the village?'

'No. I just drove straight through.'

'What was the purpose of your visit, Mr Gold?'

'To find the village.'

'Nothing more than that?'

'No, just to locate the village.'

'On this first visit. Where *did* you stay?'

'I've already said. I drove straight . . .'

'No. I mean that night? The night before your first visit to the village?'

'Oh — er — Bordfield Railway Hotel.'

'Where you're staying at the moment?'

'Yes.' Gold nodded, but instinctively I knew he'd said something he regretted. I could feel him tense a little. I glanced at him and saw the hint of worry in his eyes.

Blayde said, 'When was this? The date? Bearing in mind that Miller was killed on the Wednesday, October 15th.'

'Monday. Tuesday.' There was a hoarseness which hadn't been there before.

'Under your own name?' asked Blayde.

'Yes.' Gold nodded.

Tallboy placed his ballpoint alongside his foolscap, pushed himself up from his chair, smiled and said, 'Excuse me. I — er — I won't be moment.'

Blayde leaned back in his chair, grinned then passed cigarettes round. It was a nice act. It might have fooled a lot of people; for all I knew it was fooling both Armstrong and Gold. But as for me? It *worried* me.

Few men reach the rank of chief superintendent on the strength of foolishness. Certainly these two hadn't. They'd worked together before. Years before I'd watched Bradman and Ponsford occupy the wicket at Headingly Cricket Ground; two men, each in perfect tune with the other; virtually unbeatable; they'd stayed at the crease all day and, despite being opposed by one of the finest fielding teams of that era, the impression was that they could, had they wished, stay at the crease forever. Nobody who saw that particular match — that particular partnership — will ever forget the immaculate ease with which they dealt with the wiles of the opposition.

I was reminded of that Bradman/Ponsford partnership.

Without saying so in as many words, Tallboy had conveyed the impression that he had excused himself in order to empty his bladder. But I knew he hadn't. Squad cars were parked outside the Incident Centre; squad cars with officers ready to do whatever bidding was required.

Meanwhile we smoked cigarettes, talked about unimportant things like the weather and I tried to keep my worry from my expression.

SIX

'Did you know Annie Miller?'

Tallboy had returned and picked up his ballpoint pen. We were still smoking cigarettes, and Blayde had taken up the interrogation once more.

'No.' Gold seemed to have regained his earlier composure.

'You *didn't* know her?'

I murmured, 'He's already answered the question, superintendent.'

'Quite.' Blayde smiled. 'It seems strange, that's all, that he didn't even *know* her, I mean.'

'Her real name wasn't Annie Miller,' said Gold.

'Really?'

'Helena Schnitzler. That was her *real* name.'

'Helena Schnitzler?' If it came as a surprise, Blayde was professional enough to hide the fact. He seemed to roll the name around his tongue; as if flavouring and testing it for taste. 'Helena Schnitzler?'

'She was a wardress at Belsen. A close friend of Irma Grese.'

'Irma Grese?' Blayde frowned. I gave him the benefit of the doubt; perhaps he *didn't* remember the woman who'd earned herself the name of 'The Beast of Belsen.'

'She was tried for crimes against humanity in November, 1947. At Luneburg. She was convicted. She was hanged at Hamelin at ten o'clock on the morning of December 13th. Albert Pierrepoint officiated.'

Gold rattled off the facts, parrot-fashion; as if he'd learned them by heart and wished to impress.

'But not Helena Schnitzler?' said Blayde slowly.

'She escaped.'

'Really?'

'Belsen . . .' Gold swallowed, as if trying to control his emotions, then started again. 'Belsen was something the occupying armies hadn't expected. There was a certain amount of shock. Some . . .

pandemonium. Disbelief. Schnitzler escaped before things could be properly organised.'

'But not Grese?'

'No . . . Grese was convicted, then hanged.'

Blayde steepled his forefingers, then asked, 'Had she not escaped, would Schnitzler have been tried, convicted and hanged?'

'Don't answer that question,' I snapped. Then to Blayde, 'I can't allow my client to answer purely conjectural questions, superintendent.'

'Was he at Belsen?' Blayde switched his attention to me.

'Of course not.'

'Did he know Irma Grese?'

'Superintendent, I've already . . .'

'It seems,' crooned Blayde, 'that at least some of his remarks can already be described as 'conjectural' . . . don't you think?'

'Only in so far as recorded history is 'conjectural',' I countered. 'Evidence is available. Witnesses are available. That evidence — those witnesses — will be produced at the right time, in the right place.'

Blayde smiled a cold smile, shrugged, then turned to Gold and said, 'You're a Jew, Mr Gold. Am I right?'

Gold nodded.

'What happened at Belsen. What happened at all the other camps. Does it still upset you?'

'Doesn't it upset *you*?' It was the wrong answer, given in the wrong tone, but in honesty I couldn't blame Gold.

Blayde said, 'I like to think it justified a war, Mr Gold.'

'It did.'

'And . . . murder?' Blayde sprang the trap beautifully.

'Don't answer that question.' I had to jump in, before Gold convicted himself out of his own mouth. Then to Blayde, 'This questioning ceases, superintendent, if you insist upon asking for opinions rather than facts.'

'A fact that I have to ask, then.' Blayde smiled across the table at Gold. 'Did you kill Annie Miller? Or, if you like, did you kill the woman you claim to have been Helena Schnitzler?'

'There should be an Official Caution, superintendent,' I murmured.

'Is that necessary with you present?' Blayde's eyes stayed on Gold's face as he asked me the question.

'The Judges Rules think so,' I reminded him.

'Very well.' Then Blayde intoned, 'Samuel Gold. My name is Blayde. Detective Chief Superintendent Blayde. I must tell you that certain questions are about to be asked. You are under no obligation whatever to answer those questions. Indeed, you are not obliged to say anything unless you wish to do so, but whatever you say will be taken down in writing by my colleague, Chief Superintendent Tallboy and, in the event of your being charged with any crime, subsequent upon your answers to those questions, whatever you say may be given in evidence.' He paused, then asked, 'Do you understand what I've just said, Gold?'

'Yes, sir.' Gold nodded.

'If you *don't* understand — if you've any doubt whatever — you're at liberty to ask for an explanation. From me. From Mr Whitehouse. From your solicitor, Mr Armstrong.'

Armstrong said, 'He understands.'

'Gold?' Blayde raised questioning eyebrows.

'Yes, sir, I understand.'

Blayde turned to me, and said, 'Satisfied, Mr Whitehouse?'

'Quite satisfied, Chief Superintendent Blayde.'

Just for a moment our eyes met. It had been the first real clash, and Blayde hadn't liked it too much. I'd thrown him back on strict law and, at a guess, Blayde wasn't happy when straitjacketed within every rule and every regulation available. It was his weakness, and I'd made him show it. The eyes were narrowed slightly. Not in anger, but in realisation; in what I think was a re-appraisal. The rank didn't intimidate me . . . and that was something he wasn't used to.

Slowly — quite deliberately — he moved his head until he was staring into Gold's eyes.

He said, 'The question can now be asked. Did you kill Annie Miller?'

'No.' Gold's voice was soft, but quite steady.

'Helena Schnitzler?' He made it sound like a game. His voice lilted a shade higher at the end; a guessing game, played with some quick-witted child.

'That was her real name,' said Gold gently.

'Did you kill *her*?'

'I was responsible for her death.'

The words — the phrase — had been carefully thought out. He spoke it in a voice with little expression.

'Meaning you killed her?' pressed Blayde.

'I was responsible for her death,' repeated Gold.

'You claim that Annie Miller wasn't her real name? That her real name was Helena Schnitzler?'

'Her real name was Helena Schnitzler.'

'That she was once a friend of Irma Grese?'

'Yes.'

'That can be proved,' I added.

'That she was once a wardress at Belsen concentration camp?'

'Yes.'

I said, 'That also can be proved.'

Blayde ignored my remarks. He was the complete professional. As far as he was concerned, only Gold mattered for the moment. Armstrong, Tallboy, myself . . . we were necessary appendages. Mild annoyances imposed by The Law. We didn't *mean* anything.

He said, 'You're a Jew, Mr Gold.'

'I am.'

'This Helena Schnitzler — this woman who was a wardress at Belsen — she represented a regime which murdered six million of your fellow Jews.'

Gold nodded.

'Is that correct?' insisted Blayde.

'Murdered. Tortured. Humiliated.' Gold muttered the words from behind closed teeth.

'Therefore, she deserved to die?'

'Conjecture,' I interrupted, in a voice which refused denial. 'I can't allow . . .'

'Damn it! Keep your legal niceties for your courtroom, Whitehouse.' The passion of the explosion shocked me a little. 'I *saw* those damned camps. I *smelled* them. I saw the poor bastards crawling around among their own dead. I'll answer my own question, if you like. Yes! They deserved to die . . . every last one of 'em.' He seemed to grab his raging anger then, in a quieter voice, added, 'I've a job to do, Whitehouse. Sometimes it's a particularly foul job, but it's mine, and I do it.'

I found myself saying, 'I'm sorry, superintendent. I didn't know.'

There was a silence. A long silence in which — or so it seemed — we each lived with our own share of a guilt which embraced the whole human race. It was eerie and worrying; that we five should be so concerned about the death of one woman — and a woman who, as we believed, had once personified evil itself — while from a thousand unmarked graves more men, more women, more children than we could even visualise screamed silently for a justice which could never be theirs.

Armstrong cleared his throat, then said, 'Shall we — er — continue?'

Blayde squashed what was left of his cigarette into the ash-tray with unnecessary savagery, then growled, 'The same question, then. Who the hell she was . . . did *you* kill her, Gold?'

'I was responsible for her death.' Gold mouthed the agreed remark for the third time.

I said, 'That's as far as he's going, superintendent. He was . . . "responsible".'

'It doesn't mean much,' complained Blayde.

Gold smiled — a sad, resigned smile — as he broke the impasse. He said, 'She met her death with piano wire.'

Blayde nodded. It had been a statement of fact, but Blayde had mistaken it for a question.

'This.' Gold took a wallet from the inside pocket of his jacket and, from the wallet, slipped a small rectangle of paper. 'The receipt for the piano wire.'

'*The* piano wire?' Blayde's eyes widened as he lifted the tiny piece of paper.

'Bought in London,' said Gold.

'The piano wire with which you killed her?'

'The piano wire on which she died,' corrected Gold.

SEVEN

Tactics. Blayde and Tallboy may have thought otherwise, but we were not playing a game of 'police baiting'. That would have been very non-productive and not a little dangerous. Every move had been worked out very carefully. Every possible twist and turn of the questioning had, we hoped, been taken into account. As long as Gold's nerve held we had a case. We even had a *good* case. Our agreed tactics, however, included the convincing of Blayde that we had no case worthy of the name.

He pressed the questioning about the piano wire but, other than that it *was* piano wire — a receipt for piano wire, similar to that with which the woman had been found hanged — that was as far as he got.

'You used it?'

'I *bought* it.'

'Okay — you bought it — then you used it as a means of hanging Annie Miller?'

Gold smiled and repeated, 'I was responsible for her death.'

'By hanging her with this piano wire?'

'My client will not make a direct admission, superintendent,' I said. 'To do so would deny us any hope of a 'Not Guilty' plea.'

Blayde's lips moved into a slow, slightly twisted, grin and he said, 'Let's go back to your visits to Rimstone. Four visits . . . right?'

'This is my fourth visit.'

'The first visit. To find the place?'

'Yes.'

'When was that? The date?'

'Sunday, October 12th. In the afternoon.'

'And the second visit?'

'The next day. Again in the afternoon.'

'Monday, October 13th?'

'Yes.'

'The purpose of that visit?'

'To verify where Schnitzler lived.'

'By 'Schnitzler' you mean Annie Miller?'

'Her true name was Helena Schnitzler.'

'As you wish.' Blayde nodded brief agreement. 'Who did you ask?'

'Ask?'

'The address . . . who did you ask for the address?'

'I knew the address. I merely wanted to *find* it.'

'Okay. Who did you ask for directions?'

'Superintendent, it is a small village. I walked around. I found it without difficulty.'

'And the third visit?' asked Blayde gently.

'Thursday morning. Just after midnight.'

'While she was still alive?'

Gold nodded.

'Was she still alive?' insisted Blayde.

'Yes.'

'And when you left?'

'She was dead.'

Blayde nodded slowly. I watched his face. It registered nothing. No surprise, no triumph, no satisfaction. Nothing.

He mused, 'After midnight?'

'Shortly after midnight,' said Gold.

'How did you get into the house?'

'She was expecting us.'

I closed my eyes. I think I sent up a quick prayer. I know my heart seemed to skip a beat. But it was of no avail . . . Blayde had spotted it.

'*Us?*' he snapped.

'One of us.' Gold tried to make amends.

'One of *who?*'

'No!' I jumped in, before Gold could speak.

' '*Us*' . . . plural.' Blayde moved his head and looked at me.

'An organisation devoted to tracking down war criminals,' I explained.

'Which organisation?' The battle had shifted; it was now between Blayde and myself.

'It has no specific name.'

'Just . . . 'Us'?' he mocked, gently.
'To those within its ranks.'
'And to us, the unfavoured?'
'I don't know.'
'Mr Whitehouse.' Blayde spoke politely. A little too politely. It was a form of subtle sarcasm. 'We, the police, rarely have the privilege of talking to a Queen's Counsel across a table like this. But when we *do*, we know somebody is footing the bill. Your bill. This mysterious 'organisation', presumably?'
'Presumably,' I agreed with matching politeness.
'Are you suggesting you don't know?'
'I'm suggesting it's none of your business.'
'At the moment . . .' He sighed. 'At the moment murder is my business, Mr Whitehouse. Murder and the detection of that murder. The name of this — er — 'organisation' is of some importance.'
'I think not,' I smiled.
'I can't agree.'
'With respect, does that matter?'
We smiled at each other for a moment. Nor were the smiles false. I respected the man; he was one of the very few police officers I'd met who truly *wasn't* intimidated by the presence of a member of the Bar. And, without being falsely modest, I think he respected me . . . as a man, not as a Q.C.
I said, 'Superintendent, my client has come here freely. I venture to suggest that if he *hadn't* come forward you might have had extreme difficulty in tracing your murderer.'
'Perhaps.' The smile broadened a little. A twinkle flickered at the back of his eyes, as he added, '*Was* he the murderer?'
'He was responsible for her death.' I allowed my own smile to broaden a little.
'As far as you'll go?' he sighed.
'As far as we'll go,' I agreed.
He almost chuckled. Then he passed cigarettes round and, when we were all smoking again, he reached out a hand. He pulled a wooden box which had been to one side of the surface of the table and positioned it between himself and Gold.
He said, 'We found this buried in her garden.'

He opened the lid and I, for one, was momentarily speechless. I had rarely seen such obvious wealth packed, higgeldy-piggledy, within such a small space. I glanced at Gold and saw his face frozen in an expression unlike anything I had ever seen before. Somewhere, deep inside, was a fury which threatened to tear him apart; a white-hot rage which, while encased within layer upon layer of other emotions, tore its way to the surface and refused to be completely hidden. But the other emotions were equally strong. Heartbreak; the heartbreak of a whole nation, decimated by raving lunatics. Mourning for the millions of dead and tortured, allied to near-disbelief that such inhumanity could ever be possible. Bitterness that the world had allowed the foulness to go unchecked and, thereafter, so soon forgotten. All this plus that unique, Old Testament acceptance of a monumentally unfair fate which, in some inexplicable way, is the very touchstone of the Jewish faith. Tears spilled and rolled down his cheeks. Slowly he stretched out a hand and touched the treasure inside the box. Just touched it — didn't handle it — just touched it, as if lovingly paying homage to The Ark of The Covenant itself.

His voice was a harsh, whispered groan as he said, 'You think she *deserved* to live?'

I noted that Tallboy did not record this remark, and my respect for this officer increased a hundredfold.

Gold withdrew his hand and Blayde gently closed the lid of the box.

Blayde said, 'I think your client needs a few moments in which to compose himself, Mr Whitehouse.' He pushed his chair back and stood up from the chair. 'Let me know when he's ready, please.'

'I'm obliged.'

I was surprised to find my own voice low and hoarse with emotion.

Armstrong and Gold stood at the open door of the hall. Although they were beyond earshot, I could see they spoke little. Tallboy had disappeared towards what I took to be the vicarage and, while Blayde and I conversed quietly in one corner of the Incident Centre, I saw him return with a beaker filled with what looked like steaming hot tea, which he handed to Gold.

The thought struck me. Sometimes our policemen really *are* 'wonderful'. Throughout my life I have had much dealing with them and, in the main, they are of a breed. There are exceptions — there are *always* exceptions — but, generally speaking, they possess something which no other law-enforcement organisation in the world possesses. It is, I think, that gentleness which is a concomitant of true strength. Even Blayde. A ruthless man, a hard man, a man who (at a guess) fought without either giving or expecting quarter. Yet even he possessed that 'something'.

We smoked. We talked.

'I'm pleased I'm not a Jew,' he said gruffly.

'You saw it?' I asked.

'Some of it. Not the worst. But enough.'

'Why?' I sighed, then repeated, 'In God's name *why*?'

He knew what I meant. For the moment we were not Q.C. and senior police officer; we were two men, of an age and of an experience, and trying to understand something we both knew we could never fully understand. Nothing had been said about our conversation being 'off the record'. Nothing needed saying. We'd both just witnessed an intelligent man being threaded through a mental shredding machine. In books, in a cinema, on the television screen that would have been the moment of triumph; the moment when the police would have turned the screw and obtained a full and complete confession . . . about *anything*.

'Evil,' mused Blayde.

'It was certainly evil,' I agreed.

'No, I don't mean that . . . not exactly.' He moved the hand holding the cigarette in a vague, helpless gesture. 'The *fact* of evil . . . that's what I mean. Like goodness. Martin Luther King. Gandhi. Schweitzer. Christ, if you like . . . religion apart. Others — maybe lesser men — like Dick Sheppard. *Good* men. Men *and* women . . . maybe more women than men, if there was a head-count. People. The run-of-the-mill types — like you and me — we aren't fit to lick their boots. We can try. But we can never be like them. They have that touch of magic. Goodness. Not do-goodery, not that crap. *Goodness*. And when they're around, ordinary people feel cleaner. Better. More decent. As if — as if it's . . . contagious.' The hand moved again, and I was aware that this man was unburdening himself in a rare way. He continued, 'I once saw Sheppard. I was a kid in London . . . St Martin's-in-the-Fields. He wasn't a cleric. A preacher. He wasn't just *that*. That wasn't why the place was crowded. It was *him*.' He paused, then said, 'Remember 'Romany'?'

' 'Children's Hour',' I smiled. ' 'Uncle Eric'. 'Aunty Doris'. 'Toytown'.'

'Aye.' He nodded, and his eyes gazed into the nostalgic past. ' 'Romany', he was a cleric. He once came up North, here. A sort of lecture tour. Leeds — I saw him at one of the churches on the outskirts of Leeds. A weekday it was. One evening. It wasn't a service . . . just a talk. No dog-collar. Just ordinary clothes. Open-necked shirt. The place was full, standing-room only. Remember his dog — the spaniel — Raq?'

'And his horse. Comma.'

'Aye, because it always walked so slowly it seemed to be about to come to a full stop all the time.'

'Is that why?' I hadn't known, but knowing the man of whom we spoke, I should have guessed.

'He explained.' Blayde smiled a sad, faraway smile. 'That evening at Leeds. He even had Raq with him.'

'In church?'

'In the vestry. He brought him out at the end of his talk. Up there, a couple of yards in front of the altar. Didn't seem out of place. A beautiful dog. But — y'see — 'Romany' . . . like Dick Sheppard. That aura. That atmosphere. Not 'godliness', that's too trite. *Goodness*. Decency, plus. You could feel it. It had an effect. Okay, the effect wore off after a few days. But it was *there*.'

He drew deeply on his cigarette, frowned — probably at his own temerity in opening up so much to a complete stranger — then allowed the cigarette smoke to drift from his nostrils, before continuing, 'The same with evil, that's my opinion. Out and out bastards. They're few and far between. Most people have *some* conscience. But just occasionally . . . somebody rotten, all the way through.

'Hitler and his crowd. That's what I'm trying to say. Maybe the first time in history. A whole gang of 'em. Evil. Not just *wrong*.

Not just a making a general cock-up . . . that's understandable. But evil. It effected a whole nation. It made a whole *people* rotten. Christ!' His mouth moved into a wry, slightly self-conscious smile. 'There has to *be* a reason. Maybe that's it.'

'I — er — I can't say I've heard that argument before,' I said. 'Not in as many words.'

'Maybe I'm wrong.'

'On the other hand . . . you could be right.'

We were back at the trestle-table. Blayde and Tallboy on one side. Gold, Armstrong and myself at the other. The lines were once more drawn, but they were softer lines. Gold had brought the beaker of tea to the table; it was half-consumed and I caught the whiff of brandy from the still warm liquid and wondered where on earth Tallboy had conjured up such a steadying drink at such short notice . . . and at the same time was appreciative of that officer's basic humanity in so doing. The box which contained the jewellery had been pushed to one side; the lid firmly closed and, as far as possible, forgotten. Gold still looked pale and a little shaken, but had recovered himself enough to meet the continued questioning.

Armstrong folded his foolscap pad to a clean sheet, as Blayde said, 'Flowers.'

'Flowers?' Gold seemed to make a conscious effort to understand.

'She had flowers,' said Blayde. 'Not much food. Plenty of dirt. No papers of any kind. But a vase of flowers. Any idea why?'

Gold shook his head.

'They were in the kitchen. Dead when we broke into the house, but, at a guess, still in some sort of bloom Thursday morning. When she let you in.'

'She opened the front door to . . . me.' Then, in an attempt to cover up the pause, when he'd almost said 'us' instead of 'me', he added, 'I didn't go near the kitchen.'

'The problem,' said Blayde slowly. 'If you're right. If she was who you say she was. Concentration camp mentality and flowers . . . they don't go together. That's what . . .'

'They *do*,' interrupted Gold.

Blayde waited for amplification.

'You see, superintendent . . .' Gold sighed at the apparent inability of the world to understand. 'Those people — those guards — those warders and wardresses . . . they weren't 'wicked'. Not by the standards they'd been brainwashed into accepting. To them we were cattle. Animals. *We weren't human beings.*' An infinitely sad smile touched his mouth. Just the ghost of a smile. He added, 'Farmers can appreciate flowers. Often do.'

'Farmers are realists,' grunted Blayde. 'Okay — they like flowers — but they don't do without food for 'em. Those flowers were *wrong*. A back-to-front priority. Accepting what you say, it still doesn't make sense.'

'We're not dealing with sense,' observed Gold.

'All right.' Blayde moved a hand, as if dismissing the problem of the flowers, then said, 'The post mortem. No bruises. No sign of a struggle.'

'She didn't struggle.'

Blayde frowned.

Gold said, Your own evidence. The post mortem findings. She *didn't* struggle.'

'Nobody heard her scream.'

'She didn't scream. She didn't protest in any way.'

'That,' said Blayde bluntly, 'takes a hell of a lot of believing.'

'Only if you use normality as a yardstick.'

'Go on,' encouraged Blayde.

'A lifetime ago, superintendent.' Gold's voice was low. It seemed to come from faraway; the distance, in time, into which his eyes seemed to be gazing. Armstrong and I exchanged glances. I think he felt as I felt; I think he felt similar spiders crawling up and down his spine. Nevertheless, he bent to his task and recorded the words, as Gold continued, 'Charity. 'The greatest of these is charity'. Not from my religion, superintendent. From yours. But true, therefore, let's be charitable. Charitable even to the memory of Helena Schnitzler. Charitable enough to accept the possibility that despite everything — despite the camps and the things she was part of at those camps — she had a conscience. Grant that, and normality falls into place.

'For a lifetime — for far longer than she'd beaten and tortured —

she lived in a community where beating and torture wasn't part of everyday existence. She'd been brainwashed . . . twice. Once before she went to the camps. Once after she'd escaped from the camps. Be charitable. Accept the possibility that, for years, she'd been imprisoned . . . *inside a camp of her own making*. That the suffering she inflicted rebounded. And more. Grant that possibility. Be charitable.'

'She couldn't have lived with herself,' muttered Blayde.

Gold moved his shoulders ever so slightly.

'She'd have committed suicide,' added Blayde.

Gold said, 'We couldn't escape from *our* camps. Maybe she couldn't escape from *hers* . . . not that easily. Grant her a conscience. Be charitable, superintendent. Perhaps there was a hell through which she had to drag herself before the purge was complete. It's possible. Accept the possibility. Why she opened the door. Why she didn't struggle. Why she didn't scream.' He paused, then added, 'Maybe I opened the gate and allowed her to escape. Maybe I was what she was waiting for. *Who* she was waiting for.'

'A Jew?' Blayde's probing question was little more than a whisper.

'If not a Jew — if not one of *the* Jews — who else?'

Blayde stared at Gold for a full thirty seconds. There was real sorrow on Blayde's face. He was a police officer, conducting an enquiry . . . and hating himself for doing his duty. It was there, written in his expression and reflected in his eyes.

His voice had dropped a semitone when he said, 'Do I take what you've said to be a confession of . . .'

'No!' Having stopped the question in mid-sentence, I cleared my throat, and said, 'My client was responsible for the death of Helena Schnitzler. That's as far as he's prepared to go, Mr Blayde. That's as far as I'm prepared to *allow* him to go.'

EIGHT

Armstrong drove me back to Lessford after we'd dropped Gold off at the Bordfield Railway Hotel. Blayde hadn't even *arrested* our client. He'd merely charged him, then bailed him to appear at the Occasional Court fixed for the next day. Charged him with murder: specifically, the murder of 'a woman known as Annie Miller'. The forensic mill had started turning, but with luck and a certain amount of court-room skill *we* might determine the speed and direction of that turn.

It was dark — it had been dusk before the interview had ended — and Armstrong drove carefully in order that we might talk as we rode.

'A good start,' he opined.

'A promising start.' I was too old a hand to admit to more than that.

'He'll make a good witness,' remarked Armstrong.

'Or an uncommonly *bad* witness.'

I could feel the car slow a little as Armstrong's foot lifted slightly; part of the startled reaction to what I'd said. I saw no reason to keep the nagging doubt to myself.

I said, 'This case. It revolves around the camps.'

'In the final analysis,' he agreed.

'Specifically Belsen.'

I could feel rather than see him nod agreement.

'Gold wasn't at Belsen,' I said. 'He assured me. In answer to Blayde's question I *said* he wasn't at Belsen.'

'No, he wasn't at Belsen,' agreed Armstrong.

'And yet he seems to know much about Belsen. This woman — this Schnitzler — *she* was a wardress at Belsen. Our case — if we have a case worthy of the name — rests upon her infamies at that particular camp. It follows, therefore, that Gold's evidence is second-hand. With a sympathetic judge, plus a little luck, we might get the bulk of it through. But a good cross-examiner will tear him to shreds.'

'I'll contact The Hunter,' said Armstrong.

'Damn The Hunter!' I was immediately annoyed with myself for the outburst. Blayde's nagging interrogation of my client had, it seemed, got under my skin. I calmed my voice and said, 'This Hunter — whoever he is — doesn't know much about English law. And that's what this case is about. Law . . . not morals. I need witnesses. People who saw Schnitzler at Belsen. People who can stand in a witness box, take the oath and say, 'I was there. This happened. That happened. I *saw* it happen.'.'

'They'll be there, sir.' Armstrong was suddenly politely cool. 'You'll have their depositions in good time. They'll be ready to give evidence at the Crown Court.'

'My boy.' The last person I wished to either hurt or upset was this young man. My respect for both him and his wife was too great. This was only a case; one more case; a legal wrangle which, despite its horrific roots, need not impose itself between our feelings for each other. I said, 'My boy, I'm not criticising. You'll do your best. In heaven's name, don't let a case – even a case as sad as this – come between the friendship . . .'

'No!'

It was almost a cry of pain. It silenced me in mid-sentence and, before I could reply, Armstrong swung the car violently to the left and into a convenient lay-by. He braked to a sudden halt, switched off the lights and engine, then wound down his window. The sheer unexpectedness of it all held me silent. I watched him turn his head away from me and suck in deep breaths of the cool evening air.

I said, 'Are you – er – unwell?'

'No.'

I accepted his word and remained silent while he composed himself. He took a cigarette case from his pocket, turned his body, snapped the case open and held it out to me. I accepted the gesture, if not as an apology – indeed, no apology was needed – but as a means of re-establishing our companionship of a few moments ago. I took a cigarette, then dipped the end into the flame of his lighter. We smoked in silence for a few seconds then, when he spoke, it was in a calm, controlled tone; the tone of an honourable man who wishes to clear up misconceptions.

He said, 'Sir, have you never asked the obvious question?'

'What question is that? To whom should I have asked it?'

'To yourself.'

'And the question?'

'Why *me*?'

'I'm sorry . . . I don't follow.'

'Reginald Armstrong. A small town solicitor. From Pendlebridge. Who's even heard of *Pendlebridge*? Much less Reginald Armstrong?'

'You do yourself an injustice. You're one of the . . .'

'These people — these people represented by the man you despise — the man who insists upon being called The Hunter . . . they have the world at their disposal. They have money, they have influence, they have *everything*. Therefore, why *me*?'

'They must have a reason,' I said carefully.

He nodded, gently, then said, 'A very good reason.'

'Which you are about to tell me. And which — presumably — you think I ought to know.'

'Ruth . . .' he began, then stopped.

I waited, conscious that, whatever it was he wished to tell me, the words were difficult to find.

'We — we love each other,' he muttered. 'More than average. Y'know, we're very special to each other.'

'There's no shame in that,' I said gently.

'She . . .' Again, he stopped, drew on the cigarette, then said, 'I had hell's own job persuading her to marry me.'

'She's a most charming . . .'

'She didn't want to marry anybody. No ties. She didn't want to *love* anybody. That's — that's not an exaggeration, sir. She didn't trust anybody enough to *allow* herself to fall in love.'

'My dear boy . . .'

'She never knew her parents,' he blurted out. 'They went into the ovens at Belsen, before she even knew them.'

'Dear God!' I breathed.

We smoked our cigarettes in silence for all of a minute. What *can* one say in such circumstances? The Armstrongs. Such a happy couple. So devoted — so *right* for each other — and in the background this terrible start in life for one of the nicest young women I'd ever met. In God's name, what *does* one say at times like that?

'That's — that's why, sir.' It was a whispered groan.

I nodded my understanding.

'Other solicitors . . .' His voice gained strength a little 'They're good. Better than I am. Scores of them, much better lawyers than I'll ever be. But — y'see . . .'

'With you, it's a crusade,' I murmured.

'With me . . .' He sighed. 'With me it's for Ruth. For the people who gave me Ruth. Against the scum who refused her the right to have parents. It's . . .' He shook his head slowly. As if the English language lacked the words with which to explain his passion. He muttered, 'We're available. Just a handful of us . . . ready when needed. Sometimes to defend. Sometimes to prosecute. Whatever.' He forced a smile. 'We even have barristers. I chose you because we've been . . . y'know.' The forced smile came and went again, and he said, 'I'm sorry, sir.'

'Sorry?'

'Getting you involved like this.'

'Why be sorry?' I quite genuinely couldn't understand.

'You'll . . .' He moved a hand. 'You'll want to withdraw from the case. That's okay. As long as we stay friends. I'll tell . . .'

'That's the last thing I want to do,' I interrupted.

'Sir?'

'This is my case, young Armstrong.' I suspect my voice was gruff as I tried to cover up the feelings which boiled up within me. 'She may be your wife, but you don't have a monopoly. Other people can like her, too. Like her very much indeed. Her parents would have been of my generation, remember. I'm not suggesting I could ever . . .' I cleared my throat. 'This is my case – our case – leave it at that.'

Very quietly he said, 'You're a good man, sir.'

'That's of no importance,' I snapped. 'Just pray that I'm a good enough barrister.'

NINE

On the Sunday I rode Pullman back to London. My appearance at the Occasional Court had been a mere formality; I'd stood up, identified myself, entered a plea of 'Not Guilty' and applied for bail. Blayde had been as good as his word. He'd said, 'The police have no objection to bail, sir', and the solitary magistrate had smiled and nodded, and said, 'In that case bail is allowed, Mr Whitehouse. Shall we say three thousand pounds? For a week? We can re-new the bail on a weekly basis, if necessary.' I'd bobbed my head, mumured, 'I'm obliged, sir,' then sat down. Armstrong could have done it with equal ease and equal success, but I was anxious to identify myself with the case as soon as possible . . . and those magical letters 'Q.C.' carried a little extra weight in a magistrate's court.

The media had made token appearance. They'd sniffed something special in the wind and they, too, wanted to be in at the start. The identification of the dead woman as 'Annie Miller' caused them no curiosity. Samuel Gold was photographed and tele-filmed as we hurried him into and out of the court but, beyond his name and the fact that he'd been charged with the crime, no other information was released.

Nevertheless, their noses were twitching. The ladies and gentlemen from 'the street' were wise in the ways of their craft. Barristers and Occasional Courts form an equation worthy of interest. Elderly ladies who live like hermits and are suddenly found strangled with piano wire, and for no good reason, suggest good copy to be fed to a news-hungry public.

I sat in the comfort of the Pullman carriage, sipped moderately decent wine and gathered my thoughts upon the subject.

My beloved *cause célèbre*. My once-upon-a-time dream. To use an expression, it had already turned to ashes in my mouth. My fight (as I saw it) was to fight law with justice; to ensure that Gold remained a free man.

Barristers (or so goes the theory) remain aloof from the true guilt or innocence of their clients. They accept a brief, then they play the forensic game of move and counter-move to the best of their ability on behalf of the man or woman they represent. Go to the Inns of Court — call at the handful of bars and eating-houses frequented by men and women who wear the wig and gown — and you will hear stories galore. The villains who still walk the streets, thanks to some ploy used with skill and timing at some court. The murderers — yes, even murderers — freed as a result of tactics calculated to swing a verdict this way or that. We of The Bar are strange animals. Success demands that we remain uninvolved; at times, sleep itself requires that our objectivity is absolute. The jury decides . . . not us.

So goes the theory . . .

I sipped wine and wished fact always tallied with theory.

The Armstrongs. Oh, those infernal walls of protocol which separate barristers from solicitors! Damnation, other than a nephew with whom I spent a few happy days each year, I had no family of my own. Most of my professional colleagues were like myself; fusty old curmudgeons with little zest for life and, apart from dry-as-dust legal jokes tattered at the edges from over-telling, no humour worthy of the name. Whereas Armstrong . . . a man with a lifetime of fight ahead of him. One day the world would know Reginald Armstrong; know him as the champion of every lost cause on earth. A young man not well acquainted with compromise. 'Guilty' or 'Not Guilty'. Those, it would seem, were the only pleas he recognised. 'Mitigating Circumstances' were beneath his dignity. The satisfaction of a reduced charge was no satisfaction to him . . . it was tantamount to a defeat.

I'd met solicitors — scores of solicitors in my life in the courts — and not one other of them would have said what Armstrong had said as we waited on Lessford Railway Station. 'He killed her, of course, but that's not the point. She deserved to die.' And he'd made it an almost off-handed remark; as if the point hardly needed mentioning, much less stressing. An unimportant conversational back-filling while we awaited the arrival of the train for London.

Nor had I been shocked. Or even surprised. Because that was what we *were* attempting . . . the acquittal of a man who, in honesty, *had* committed deliberate murder.

That, then, was how close we were. How much we trusted each other. The two of us. No! The *three* of us, because now Ruth, his wife, had become a factor. Perhaps *the* factor.

The attendant stopped at my table and asked if I would like coffee. Pâté and toast, perhaps? It seemed a good idea. I drained my glass and handed it to him, and he left me to my musings.

To defend a man you *know* to be guilty. Not, as in the past, to be unconcerned about his guilt or innocence; to accept his story, more or less at face value, thereafter to hope he's told you enough of the truth to form a reasonable defence. Not that, this time. To fight for what you *know* to be a wrong verdict. Because of circumstances, because a megalomaniac had ruled almost all Europe a lifetime ago, because I had an affection for a young solicitor who, over the years, had become almost a substitute-son ... but, perhaps most of all, because of his wife.

That he'd made that remark on Lessford Station should have been enough. The barrister/solicitor relationship refused him the right to make that remark and still expect me to plead on behalf of his client. Without even giving the matter much thought I could have reeled off at least half a dozen perfectly valid and long established reasons why I should have literally thrown the brief back into his lap. And more, perhaps. By not reporting his remarks to The Law Society I was making myself liable to a monumental criticism from The Bar Council.

But — dammit — I didn't care. I was past middle-age; fast approaching the 'elder statesman' stage. This, if you will, was the reason for it all. A life of legal hair-splitting and court room battles. For this . . . one last wild and suicidal throw of the forensic dice.

And who the devil *says* a born bachelor doesn't know the meaning of paternal love?

I settled down to enjoy my coffee, my toast and my pâté.

I doubt if I'd ever felt so certain of anything in all my life.

Mind you, there was still Smith-Hopkinson ...

That evening — within thirty minutes of arriving home — I telephoned his apartment and asked him round. What I had to say to him was not for chamber gossip and, although I suspect that my call might have interrupted his somewhat involved love life, he agreed readily enough and was at my flat within the hour.

I settled him in one of the armchairs, fed him good sherry then, when we were both relaxed, I said, 'You can, I know, keep a confidence.'

'Yes. Of course, sir.' His interest quickened.

'I mean a real confidence. In effect, a secret.'

'Of course.'

I told him of Armstrong's visit to my flat, of my journey north, of my meeting with Gold, of the murder of 'Annie Miller', of the true identity of the murdered woman, of the questioning of Gold by Blayde.

I said, 'Obviously, I need a junior counsel.'

'I'd be honoured, sir.' A look of mild puzzlement went with his expected reply.

'Would you?' I murmured. 'Would you indeed?'

'Most certainly, sir. We've worked together . . .'

'The plea is 'Not Guilty'. Without qualifications.'

'I can quite understand that.' He smiled. 'Knowing Armstrong...'

'The — er — keeping of a secret.' I stared into his eyes.

He looked me in the face and waited.

'Gold murdered her,' I said flatly. 'Armstrong knows it. I know it. Now you know it. In law, we'll be fighting for what we know to be a wrong verdict.'

'Oh!' He tasted his sherry, swallowed, then tasted it again.

'You have a promising future,' I reminded him. 'One might almost prophesy a brilliant future.'

'That's very kind of . . .'

'I, on the other hand, have a very average past. I have little to lose. You have *everything* to lose. That's why you had to be told.'

'Sir.' He scowled at the surface of what was left of the sherry.

'I'm sorry,' I growled. 'I shouldn't have asked you. I've placed an intolerable burden upon our . . .'

'Sir — what I was going to say — whatever I am, whatever future I may have, is due in the main to your kindness. I'm — I'm unlike you in so many ways. I'm something of a gadfly. You're so . . . reliable.'

'Reliable'! What a description. What an accolade for years of work in the courts and in the chambers. Like an old clock that ticks away in a dark corner, keeps good time, but has little else to recommend it. The word — the description — suddenly made me feel the full weight of my years. My own crass stupidity in never even looking for some understanding woman with whom to share a rather dull and uninspiring life. I'd been a fool. Damnation, I'd been *born* old . . . old and foolish. Never once had I . . .

'I'd have been hurt — very hurt — had I not been your first choice, sir.'

'Eh?' I blinked and, like a rising blind, the dark mood rolled away to reveal ray upon ray of sunshine. 'You mean you'll accept?'

'Of course.' The scowl had been replaced by a grin. A distinctly mischievous grin. The sort of grin no rising young barrister should *ever* allow freedom of his features.

'Conspiracy to defeat the ends of justice,' I reminded him.

'I know.' The grin broadened. 'And if *we* can't do it, who can?'

'Smith-Hopkinson,' I said, 'you're a scoundrel.'

'Yes, sir.' He nodded cheerfully.

'You have no respect for the law.'

'The law, sir — as the saying goes — is an ass.'

'Sometimes,' I agreed. I pushed myself up, out of my armchair, brought the sherry bottle from its corner table and said, 'A toast, then.' I topped up our glasses, then raised mine and said, 'To the confusion of all things asinine.'

We touched glasses, then drank deeply and I prayed neither of us would regret the toast.

TRIAL

ONE

People — acquaintances whom I occasionally introduce to the creaking panoply of 'The English Legal System' in full cry — often remark upon the *smallness* of the average court room. What they expect has always puzzled me. A Roman amphitheatre, perhaps? Something on a par with The Royal Albert Hall? A court room is a place of talk; of questions and answers; of propositions and arguments. It seems obvious, therefore, that those who talk should be within easy talking *distance* of each other.

Nor — if you examine the place with some care — is the average court-room so *very* tiny. Its furniture, alone, covers an uncommon area of floor-space. The dock, the two (sometimes three) rows of seats for the barristers and solicitors, the witness box, the jury bench, the press box, the massive table upon which briefs, volumes and exhibits are put on display, the public gallery, at the rear, the raised dais, upon which sit the clerk and his assistant and, finally — towering above the lawyers and jury alike — the judge's seat ... all this, plus gangways, entrance areas and the like. Not, after all, such a *small* place.

Lessford Crown Court is one such room and, on Wednesday December 8th, it was a little like coming home. Or, if not actually coming home — Lessford being beyond the boundaries of my own circuit — at least like re-visiting a well known, although not necessarily well-loved, place of homage. God bless me, even the officials were the same as last time. Clipstone, Q.C. was prosecuting, with Abel again acting as his junior. Even the same judge; Mr Justice Belmont. It really was quite like old times.

Smith-Hopkinson and I had trained north the previous day. We'd spent the evening, almost till midnight, with Armstrong and Gold. We'd argued out the various permutations of our agreed tactics and, at the end of the session, Smith-Hopkinson had encapsulated the whole of our conclusions in one of those ridiculous phrases mouthed by a society influenced by transatlantic idiom. 'We just hoist a few flags up the flag-pole and see who salutes which.' Gold's almost casual stoicism, on the other hand, had been very off-putting. 'I'm not important. If I go to prison, it doesn't really matter. The main thing is to let the world know who *she* was . . . and that others, like her, be made to keep glancing over their shoulders.' But, to me, that was *not* the main thing. That was only half the task I'd set myself; the other half – the problem of ensuring that Gold walked from the court a free man – was likely to be the more difficult part.

In the robing room Clipstone and I – Smith-Hopkinson and Clipstone's junior, Abel – had acknowledged each other's existence. Little more than that. The mild banter was missing. The exchange of pleasantries. The tacit understanding that, although we were opponents within the well of the court we were, nevertheless, civilised men and capable of friendship outside the confines of the case.

And now, we were *in* the well of the court. Wigs and gowns had been donned, the pink ribbon of the briefs had been untied and a court official was guiding the jurors to their places on our right.

'Do we challenge?' murmured Smith-Hopkinson.

I glanced at the jurors. Nine men, three women. I played the usual guessing game. Two of the women looked to be housewives; one of them at the *Woman's Own* level, the other slightly more assured at (say) the *Homes and Gardens* level. The third woman looked spinsterish; either sour-faced or frightened . . . I couldn't decide which, but gave her the benefit of the doubt.

'We need the women,' I said, in a low voice. 'If we have tears, we must be prepared to shed them.'

Smith-Hopkinson smiled at my atrocious mis-quote of the bard.

The male members of the jury? The man who was obviously going to end up as foreman; a large, squarely-built man; a man used to having his own way; florid-faced, Harris-tweeded and, without much doubt a fervent member of the 'Hang-'em-and-flog'em' crowd. Certainly old enough to have served in Hitler's war; possibly as an officer. Of the other eight men, I estimated that five – possibly six – had also seen, or been part of, that same war. They *knew* . . . they didn't have to be told. The remaining two men? At least they wore shirts and ties; we hadn't medallions or worry-beads to contend with.

I took the first gamble. I said, 'We don't challenge. If we can't get them all, there's always a majority verdict.'

Smith-Hopkinson nodded his understanding.

From behind me Armstrong leaned forward and whispered, 'Pity there isn't a Jew amongst them.'

I turned my head sideways, and whispered, 'If we challenge, unnecessarily, we show our hand before the case even begins.'

'Nevertheless . . .'

'The non-Jews were responsible,' I argued. 'Hopefully, somewhere in that jury there's an unconscious guilt-complex. If we play on *that* . . .'

Armstrong grunted. He wasn't quite convinced but, on the other hand, he lacked my experience as far as juries were concerned.

The great mystique of The Jury System . . .

I tell you, out of every twelve there are always at least six — more often as many as eight — to whom jury service is an infernal nuisance. It interferes with their life, it interferes with their work and, in the main, they want the thing over and done with as soon as possible. They grow bored and irritable, long before the end of the case. When they retire, they go along with the rest; they don't argue, they don't think, they don't *care*. Their vote — if you can call it a vote — is based upon convenience rather than upon guilt or innocence. The trick, therefore, is to pick out the one — perhaps the two — who *do* care. Who *will* argue. Ignore the others . . . they'll be led, when the time arrives. Merely ensure that they'll be led in the required direction.

The clerk of the court edged his way along the front of his desk. He was a stout man. Obese. A Pickwickian figure whose bulging stomach had to be eased below the rim of the desk as he lowered himself into his chair. His assistant followed him and, by contrast, he was a 'lean and hungry fellow'. I was reminded of the characters, Weary Willie and Tired Tim; cartoon figures from the now defunct children's weekly *Chips* which, as a tot, I'd read avidly, having smuggled it into the disapproving atmosphere of prep school.

There followed the usual to-ing and fro-ing, up-ing and down-ing and, eventually Mr Justice Belmont was settled in his seat of office, the members of the jury had been sworn in and Gold was in the dock, facing his accusers.

The trial was under way.

Clipstone opened for the Prosecution.

Clipstone, be it clearly understood, was a most excellent barrister. He took his profession seriously and, because of that, he did what he was required to do ... and nothing more. The sad fact is that some barristers – far too many barristers! – forget that Prosecuting Counsel is not required to *fight*. Indeed, as has been emphasised on appeal, he is not even entitled to. His task is merely to assist the jury in arriving at the truth; no more, no less. In effect (and a fact rarely appreciated by the public and, sadly, equally not clearly understood by many of my fellow members of The Bar) a Prosecuting Counsel should never actively interest himself in the conviction of an accused person. His sole object is to ensure that the *right* person is convicted.

This, of itself, gives the Defending Counsel a distinct edge. The Defence is not merely *allowed* to fight; it is their duty to fight. By every legal means available they are expected to destroy the suggestion that the person they represent is the right person to convict. Even *might* not be the right person is enough ... The presumption of innocence does the rest.

Thus, the law. But the reality is that, in some cases, too many jurors start with what might be termed 'the presumption of guilt'. The firmly held belief that, because the police have placed the prisoner in the dock then, almost by definition, the prisoner should be convicted. So many excuses. 'He wouldn't be there, if he hadn't done it.' 'The police know more than they're allowed to tell.' 'If we let him get away with it, we'll be letting the police down.'

As Clipstone made his scrupulously fair opening address I glanced at the jury and wondered, when they retired, how many of them would voice those, or similar, remarks.

As Clipstone lowered his papers, prior to calling his first witness, I rose to my feet and fired my opening shot.

'My lord,' I said with almost fawning respect.

Belmont raised his eyes questioningly.

I said, 'My learned friend has used the name 'Annie Miller' when speaking of the dead woman. That name also appears on the indictment.'

'Well?' Belmont knew how to drop a word like a stone down an unused pit-shaft.

'My lord, the Defence will bring positive proof that 'Annie Miller' was not, in fact, her name. That her real name was Helena Schnitzler and that, by birth, she was German.'

'Does that make her any less dead?' Belmont didn't like this early introduction of what he might have called 'unessentials'.

I said, 'It is of some importance to the Defence, my lord.'

'Really?'

'And — with respect — it is a fault in the indictment. A very fundamental fault.'

Clipstone had resumed his seat. He was switching his gaze between Belmont and myself. A faint smile touched his lips as the judge and I crossed swords.

Belmont sniffed his displeasure and said, 'Of importance to the Defence, you say?'

'I would wish the trial to continue, my lord,' I murmured politely.

'Eh?'

He took my meaning. Of course he did. I could, had I wished, have stopped the trial; have insisted upon a complete re-drafting of the indictment, going all the way back to the committal proceedings and beyond. In truth, I could have made a monumental nuisance of myself and Belmont knew it. Nor would Belmont himself have been free from criticism. Harry Truman's well-known dictum 'The buck stops here' is equally applicable to Crown Court judges. They carry the final responsibility for whatever goes on in their own court; that they delegate much of their responsibility is both true and necessary, but they can never abdicate that responsibility. I 'had' him, he didn't like being 'had', but there was nothing he could do about it.

He cleared his throat, then said, 'Do I take it, Mr Whitehouse, that you are agreeable to an amendment to the indictment, as it stands?'

'As you see fit, my lord.' I bobbed my head.

'I do so see fit.'

He leaned forward, tapped the clerk of the court on top of his wig with the silver ballpoint pen he was using, and that worthy forced himself upright, turned and, I have no doubt, received the whispered rough edge of Belmont's tongue.

In my own ear Armstrong's voice breathed, 'Was that wise, sir? We may have antagonised the judge. We may have to pay for it.'

I leaned back in my chair and, *sotto voce*, said, 'Armstrong, old chap, leave the tactics to me.'

'Yes, sir. But . . .'

'We'll butter up Belmont later. For the moment we've planted a seed of doubt in the mind of the jury. The police evidence. Their enquiries. They didn't even take the trouble to find the woman's real name.'

By this time I was seated once more and Clipstone was on his feet, waiting. He glanced at me, and I thought I detected a distinct twinkle in his eyes; he knew the tricks of advocacy as well as any man and, at a guess, knew why I'd waited until this particular moment before pointing out the inaccuracy in the indictment. Things gradually settled down; the court clerk heaved himself back into his chair before passing his whispered outrage down the line to his assistant; Belmont looked cross – or, to be more accurate, crosser than usual – and, at a sign from on high, Clipstone called his first witness.

William Harper, the milk-roundsman, gave his evidence in short, sharp bursts. Twice Clipstone turned his head in my direction and, when I gave a tiny nod of acquiescence, asked deliberately leading questions. Each time Belmont gazed at me quizzically and, each time, I smiled back innocently. Gradually I was gaining his approval; Belmont – like all judges – disliked the smooth progress of a case being interrupted by unnecessary objections.

Clipstone sat down, and I rose to cross-examine.

'Just a few questions, Mr Harper.' I used a friendly enough tone, and the near-panic which had touched his expression disappeared. 'The dead woman. You knew her as Mrs Miller? Or, perhaps, *Miss* Miller?'

'Yes, sir. Annie Miller.'

'Did she answer to that name?'

'Er — no, sir. She . . .'
'What name did she answer to?'
'Well — er — she didn't, sir.'
'She didn't?'
'We — we never spoke, sir.'
'Not once? In — how long was it? — three . . .'
'Nearly three years, sir.'
'Not a word passed?'
'No, sir.'
'Not a solitary greeting?'
'Nothing, sir.'
'Strange,' I mused. Then in the form of a question, 'Strange . . . wouldn't you agree?'
'She was a strange woman, sir.'
That's what I needed. An opinion, as opposed to a bald statement of fact. Harper, as a witness, was unimportant; unimportant enough to allow me to coax an opinion from him, without any objection from Clipstone. But, having obtained one opinion, I could use that opinion as a question to other, more important witnesses.

I said, 'In what way did you find her strange, Mr Harper?'
'Like — like a hermit, sir.'
'A hermit?'
'Secretive. Y'know . . . as if she'd summat to hide.'
'You, of course, didn't know *what* she had to hide?'
'No, sir.'
'Nor that her *real* name was Helena Schnitzler?'
'No, sir. I didn't know that, either.'
'Thank you, Mr Harper.'

I sat down. Belmont looked at Clipstone for some indication as to whether there was to be a re-examination or not. Clipstone shook his head, and Harper left the witness box.

The next witness to take the stand was Police Constable 1781 Samuel Henry Stone. As Clipstone took him through the evidence in chief I tried to size the man up. Solid, stolid and dependable. That was the intended impression. But his weakness? He'd been in too many witness boxes; he 'knew the ropes' . . . or thought he did.

Every answer was pat, too pat. He was too accurate by far and, as an aide memoire, his notebook was open on the ledge of the box.

'Demolish him.' I whispered the words into Smith-Hopkinson's ear. 'In the nicest possible way, of course.'

Smith-Hopkinson nodded. For a moment a grin, like that of a hungry tiger, touched my junior's lips. His was the task of inserting the first wedge into the edifice of the police structure, and he obviously relished the task.

As Clipstone sat down, Smith-Hopkinson rose, paused as if unable to find *any* question worthy of the name 'cross-examination' — a neat touch! — then murmured, 'You — er — you were the first police officer to see the dead woman . . . is that correct, constable?'

'Yes, sir.'

'At — er . . .' Smith-Hopkinson consulted his notes. 'At seven-forty-seven, on the morning of Sunday, October 19th?'

'Yes, sir.'

'Having received the telephone call, at your home, at seven-twelve?'

'Yes, sir.'

'You were in bed at the time?'

'Yes, sir. I'd been on late shift.'

'Now — let me see — er — Rimstone Beat . . . am I right?'

'Yes, sir. Rimstone Beat. Part of Sopworth Section.'

'Sopworth Section?'

For a moment, I felt a twinge of sympathy for the uniformed constable in the witness box. He was being played like a fish. The slightly 'silly ass' tone in which Smith-Hopkinson was (seemingly) stumbling through unimportant questions was sheer craftsmanship. The constable obviously thought himself well able to handle *this* sort of questioning. Indeed, his mouth moved slightly as he tried to control that self-satisfied smile which comes only with complacency.

He said, 'Sopworth Section, sir. Part of Bordfield Division. Rimstone Beat . . . that's part of Sopworth Section.'

'You live on the beat? At Rimstone?'

'Oh, yes sir. It's an outside beat.'

'Outside?'

'Detached, sir. Not worked from any police station.'

'Oh, I see.' Smith-Hopkinson's grin was pure P.G.Wodehouse. 'You live at Rimstone. You patrol Rimstone. You — er — you must have known the dead woman.'

'No, sir.'

'Why not?' smiled Smith-Hopkinson innocently.

'I — er — I just didn't, sir. Mrs Miller was a bit of a . . .'

'Who?'

'Mrs Miller, sir. She was . . .'

'Oh! You mean Helena Schnitzler?'

'Yes, sir. I suppose I do.' Stone smiled at the jury.

'Then why not *call* her Helena Schnitzler?'

'It's just that . . .' Stone began to flounder a little. He no longer smiled at the jury.

'You didn't *know* her name was Helena Schnitzler?' suggested Smith-Hopkinson.

'No, sir. I — er — didn't know.'

'Whereas you *did* know her name was "Annie Miller"?'

'Er — yes, sir.'

'You *knew* that?' pressed Smith-Hopkinson.

'Sir?'

'That her name was "Annie Miller"?'

'Well, sir, no . . . I didn't exactly *know*.'

'Then,' droned Belmont, 'In God's name why say you *did* know?'

'M'lord?' Stone's face was beginning to shine a little.

'In answer to counsel's question — a very simple, straightforward question — you assured the court that you *did* know the woman. More than that. That you knew her name *was* "Annie Miller".'

'No, m'lord. I — er — I didn't say . . .'

'I have a note of your answer here, constable.' Belmont tapped his open notebook. 'You were asked whether you *knew* her name was "Annie Miller" and your reply was a categorical "Yes".'

'I — I didn't mean that, m'lord.'

'It would,' said Belmont sarcastically, 'assist the court considerably, constable, if you said what you meant . . . or, on the other hand, meant what you said. Don't you think?'

Stone groaned, 'Yes, m'lord. I'm — I'm sorry, m'lord.'

Smith-Hopkinson's smile was almost apologetic as he continued to gently crucify the now sweating Constable Stone.

He said, 'The name 'Annie Miller'. Can the court take it that what you mean is that you knew the dead woman *by* that name?'

'Yes, sir,' breathed Stone. 'That's — that's exactly . . .'

'But that you have no reason to doubt that her real name was Helena Schnitzler?'

'N-no reason at all, sir.'

'Why . . .' Smith-Hopkinson cleared his throat quietly. 'Why did you know her by the name of 'Annie Miller', constable?'

'I'd — I'd been told that that was her name, sir.'

'By whom?'

'The other villagers, sir.'

'Specifically?'

'Sir?'

'The people — the person — who told you that was her name?'

'The — er . . . Her friends, sir. The people who knew her.'

'Indeed?' That fractional rise of the eyebrows was perfect. As was the small pantomime of shuffling through the papers, as though verifying some half-forgotten fact. 'She's been described as . . . I'm referring to Helena Schnitzler, of course. She's been described as a hermit. As being secretive.' He raised his head and asked 'Who *were* her friends, constable?'

'I dunno, sir,' muttered Stone.

'I beg your pardon?'

'I don't know who her friends were, sir.'

'People who knew her then?'

'Not many . . .' Stone swallowed, then blurted, 'I don't think anybody actually *knew* her, sir.'

'Therefore when people told you her name was 'Annie Miller'?'

'I — I accepted it, sir.'

'You took it on trust?'

'Yes, sir.'

'You seem,' said Smith-Hopkinson severely, 'to have taken rather a lot on trust . . . don't you?'

'I — I wouldn't say . . .'

'That she was a Jewess, for example?'

Stone didn't answer.

Smith-Hopkinson snapped, 'Who first suggested that Helena Schnitzler was a Jewess?'

'I – er ...'

'This!' Smith-Hopkinson held the headlined newspaper with a flourish. '*Jewish woman slain in ritual murder*,' he quoted. 'Who first suggested she was a Jewess. And,' he warned, 'the Defence *has* caused certain enquiries to be made.'

Stone swallowed, then breathed, 'The missus.'

'Who?'

'My – my wife, sir.'

'Your *wife*?'

'Yes, sir. I – er – I passed it on like.'

'To whom?'

'Sir?'

'To whom did you convey this priceless, albeit inaccurate, piece of information?'

'To – to Chief Superintendent Tallboy, sir.'

'Your wife knew the dead woman, presumably?'

'No, sir. Like I've said ...'

'She *didn't* know her?'

'No, sir. No ... she didn't know her, sir.'

'In that case ...'

'She'd – she'd heard her talk, sir.'

'Indeed?'

'In a supermarket, once, sir. Y'know ... in a supermarket.'

'Just the once?'

'Yes, sir.'

'A long conversation, presumably?'

'No, sir. Just passing the time of day, like.'

'I see.' Smith-Hopkinson hoisted his gown more firmly across his shoulders, in the approved manner, then said, 'Your wife is a dialectician, is she?'

'Sir?'

'Skilled in various dialects?'

Belmont droned, 'The word is 'dialectologist'.'

'I'm obliged my lord.' Smith-Hopkinson bobbed his head. Then, to Stone, 'Your wife, constable. Is she a dialectologist?'

'Er . . . no, sir.'

'In that case . . .' Smith-Hopkinson spread his palms in mock amazement.

Belmont frowned at the wretched Stone, and asked, 'Is this court to understand that your wife — no expert in such matters and on the strength of a few words exchanged in some supermarket — expressed the opinion that the dead woman was a Jewess, that you, in turn passed that opinion on to a senior police officer and that on the strength of such flimsy evidence — if, indeed, it *deserves* to be called evidence, however flimsy — the enquiry into this murder was concentrated upon lines based upon a non-existent anti-semitic motive?'

Stone's mouth opened and closed a couple of times, but no sound came from his lips.

I excused myself and, with as little fuss as possible, made my way out of the court room. The tiled corridors with their groups of waiting witnesses and jury people were another world. A much nicer world. A world wherein, figuratively speaking, horns weren't locked in mortal combat. I was about to make my way to the robing room, then changed my mind and went to the main entrance of the building. For a moment I wanted to be alone and, behind the shelter of one of the stone columns which held up the Georgian-style porch I found solitude and shelter from what little wind there was. I lighted a cigarette and, not for the first time, concerned myself with the legitimate trickery of court room conflict.

The truth is, I felt sorry for this Constable Stone. My junior was doing a first-rate job; by this time — having veered off from the obvious at the start of the cross-examination in order to distract attention — Smith-Hopkinson would, without doubt, have the constable's notebook in his hand. It had been on the ledge of the box, *ergo* it had been 'produced' in court and was available for examination by counsel. Those split-seconds timings; when he'd been called, when he'd first seen the body . . . always the same and always so stupid. No man, however good a police officer, checks the time to the minute throughout *every* step of a major crime enquiry. It can't be done. I never *is* done . . . in effect it would be like detecting crime with a stop-watch in one hand. But because police procedure demands that it *should* be done, a great pretence is played.

In my mind I could hear the questions. 'You checked the time?' 'Despite the fact that you were shocked at finding the woman apparently dead — apparently murdered — you looked at your watch and noted the *exact* time?' The minor bombardment of such questions . . . all aimed at making Stone a liar. Because he *was* a liar. Not a rogue, not even a bad police officer, but merely a liar in order to keep the 'paperwork' tidy. And the body of the notebook — away from the entries concerning this and other major incidents — to the nearest five minutes. As loosely timed as *that*. I'd given my instructions to Smith-Hopkinson. 'Demolish him.' And I knew my junior would do it.

I stood within the shelter of the column, smoked my cigarette and, not for the first time in my life, mulled over the pros and cons of criminality . . . in and out of a court room.

Perhaps I was being a little unfair, but I suspected Smith-Hopkinson of feeling far too self-satisfied.

He said, 'It really was as easy as picking apples from a barrel.'

'You did a magnificent job,' said Armstrong. 'From now on, every police witness will be suspect.'

'But not, necessarily, a liar,' I added grimly.

We were in a restaurant, within easy walking distance of the court. Belmont had adjourned the hearing for lunch, when the wretched Stone had, at last, been allowed to leave the witness box, and now we were awaiting our respective orders and, while we waited, talking over the case and its possible outcome.

'Gold?' I asked.

Armstrong said, 'He's in the cells under the court. I've arranged for a meal to be sent in to him.'

Smith-Hopkinson looked uneasy, then said, 'Sir, you told me to . . .'

'I know, 'Demolish him'. You did an excellent job.'

'In that case . . .'

'My dear boy, I'm not criticising,' I assured him. I smiled, then continued, 'Myself, perhaps. But not you.'

I could see that my attitude was dampening their own high spirits, and I was sorry. I could do little about it. They were younger men than I; a whole generation younger. Of the modern era where to win is the only thing of real importance. Whereas to me the mode of winning was of almost equal importance. Nor could I rid myself of the thought of what my colleagues might say, did they know that 'Old Man Whitehouse' had at last succumbed to fighting a case in which he didn't believe; a case in which he *knew* his client was guilty.

Shame? Personal guilt? No, that would be going too far. I was worried. That was the truth of the matter; worried about a certain middle-aged man who happened to be a police constable and who, because I'd said 'Demolish him' and because my junior knew his job, would certainly get into trouble. Might even be dismissed from the force. I didn't *think* he'd be sacked; I knew of no instance of an officer being dismissed, or even of being asked to resign, other than as a result of out-and-out perjury. And Stone hadn't committed that crime.

In a quiet voice, I said, 'I doubt whether Constable Stone will be enjoying his lunch.'

'It was necessary, sir,' said Armstrong.

'Indeed.' I nodded sad agreement. 'But I must have a quiet word with Chief Superintendent Blayde after the case. Explain the necessity.'

'You think he won't know?'

'He might. He's no fool.'

'Sir.' Smith-Hopkinson sought to comfort me. 'Remember your own advice. The jury . . . only the jury matters in the long run.'

'And,' I sighed, 'we've destroyed the credibility of police evidence. Temporarily, at least.'

And that, I fear, was as much consolation as I could seriously offer myself. Nothing self-congratulatory. Nothing of which to be particularly proud. We were fighting for Gold's freedom but, in strict law, he had no right to that freedom. And that, too, I think irked me. Saddened me. On the one hand I was prepared to accept the proposition that, of all people, Helena Schnitzler deserved the fate the man who called himself The Hunter had reserved for her. But on the other hand I had a respect for the Rule of Law which almost amounted to love.

The waiter arrived with our orders, and I forced myself to push the conflict from the front of my mind. Fatalistically — cowardly, if you will — I decided to take things witness at a time . . . and who the devil *does* know which direction any case will take?

Much of the afternoon was taken up by the evidence of the pathologist who'd performed the post mortem, followed by Dr Carr from the Forensic Science Laboratory, followed by police photographers who'd taken long-shots and close-ups of the scene and the body.

Unless one is an Edward Marshall Hall and, like that giant, blessed with both scientific and forensic expertise, it behoves an advocate to allow the experts freedom to express an opinion without serious contradiction. Good cross-examination can win cases. But *bad* cross-examination can, equally, *lose* cases, and cross-examination for the sake of cross-examination merely irritates the judge and bores the jury. After all, we were not disputing the death of Helena Schnitzler, nor even her mode of death. The where, the how, the when of her death was not in dispute. Our job — our *only* job — was to sever the link between that death and Samuel Gold. To sever it if possible or, at the least, weaken it until it could no longer stand the strain of the presumption of innocence.

Throughout that afternoon, therefore, we sat and listened; followed the evidence on the depositions from the committal court and, where necessary, made notes or underlined passages which might be of use to us later in the trial.

The afternoon ended with Blayde's evidence-in-chief. His manner in the witness box did much to retrieve what Constable Stone had lost, and both Smith-Hopkinson and myself followed his every word. The perfect witness. 'Yes, sir.' 'No, sir.' 'I don't know, sir.' The triple-curse of all cross-examiners; no qualifications upon which to hang a garland of follow-up questions designed to bind him and force an eventual contradiction. Even in the examination-in-chief Blayde used those three answers as often as possible. A straight story, with no opinion expressed one way or the other.

Clipstone sat down and, before I rose to cross-examine, Belmont glanced at the clock, checked with his own watch, then said, 'Your cross-examination of the witness tomorrow morning, Mr Whitehouse?'

It was a question, but I bobbed my head and murmured, 'I'm obliged m'lord.'

'We will adjourn for today.' Then, frowning at the jurors, 'You will not discuss this case with *anybody*. Not even amongst yourselves. You are under oath until the end of this case. If it comes to my notice that any member has broken the terms of that oath, I shall not hesitate. I shall, rightly, view it as a contempt of this court.'

TWO

That evening we dined at Pendlebridge with Armstrong and his wife. It was a curious meal; perfectly cooked and tastefully presented; served with good wine at a table whose crockery, cutlery and glassware shone and sparkled in a room beautifully furnished, delightfully illuminated. Yet (to me) a curious meal.

I am of the school — of the age — when good food and good conversation go together. When to dine out means pleasant talk; a relaxation of the spirit; a slight loosening of the tongue; an exchange of quips and opinions. When the bonds of friendship are strengthened by reason of each man and each woman revealing a fraction more of his, or her, personality than was previously known. To gather together merely to *eat* is (to me) both time-wasting and an insult to civilised conduct.

I was aware — nobody more so — that for a solicitor to act as host to a barrister (to a Q.C. *and* his junior!) midway through a case is not the 'done thing'. The relationship should be cool. Distant. And this, however close the relationship other than when that case is being heard. The mores and manners of the Bar. From time . . . when? From when tonsured monks were the 'pleaders' and wigs were introduced as a means of hiding their bald pates. From when solicitors and attorneys knew the ridiculously intricate 'forms and pleadings' but, other than that, knew little and were not fit companions for holy men. I was knowledgeable about the forensic idiocies which stretch back through the centuries, but was prepared to ignore them insofar as Armstrong and his wife were concerned. Assuming that a born bachelor ever knows the real meaning of the word 'love' that is what I felt for these two. Nor was my feeling for Smith-Hopkinson many degrees less. And I was self-opinionated enough to feel sure that there was a reciprocal affection from all three.

It should have been a happy meal.

It wasn't. The small-talk was forced. The laughter was not spontaneous. There was a fifth guest — an unseen guest — at the table, and the name of that guest was trepidation. Trepidation which almost amounted to downright fear.

As we sipped coffee and smoked, Ruth Armstrong gave it another name.

She said, 'I was in the public gallery today. Blayde. How will he stand up under cross-examination?'

'Well,' I answered bluntly.

'He thinks he holds all the cards for a conviction,' observed Smith-Hopkinson. He smiled, then added, 'The casebooks are fat with men who held the same opinion and were wrong.'

'Not many men like Blayde.' I scowled at the surface of my coffee. 'At a guess — and at this moment — he'll be toying with all the likely questions he'll be asked. He'll have the answers ready.'

'Too ready?' murmured Smith-Hopkinson. 'Too sure of himself?'

'With other men,' I grunted.

'Simon.' Ruth Armstrong was one of the few people who used my first name quite naturally, and without embarrassment either to herself or me. She said, 'Simon, you sound *afraid*.'

'My dear.' I smiled. 'Not afraid . . . worried. Very worried. I'm not a betting man, but if I were, my money would be on Blayde. Stone was easy. A good barrister . . .' I glanced at my junior. 'A good barrister could have cross-examined him out of existence. Our friend here did just that. In effect, he turned him from a police witness to a witness for the Defence.' I paused, then added, 'But that was Constable Stone.'

'And Blayde?' she asked.

'I've met Blayde.' I sighed. 'He knows the tricks. The most we can hope for is that we know some tricks he *doesn't* know.'

'We have right on our side,' said Armstrong.

'No!' Quite suddenly, quite needlessly, I was annoyed with this young solicitor. 'We have the truth on our side. *Some* of the truth ... not *all* of the truth. The whole truth would send Gold to prison.' My spat of annoyance died as quickly as it had been born. In a quieter voice, I said, 'Justice, perhaps. We have justice on our side. With what we have — with justice — we have to defeat the law.'

The talk veered away from the subject. It was a deliberate change of direction. I knew (I think we all knew) that nothing short of a miracle could save Gold from a prison sentence. Perhaps a long prison sentence. The most I could do — the most I could *hope* to do — was to press an empty plea of 'Not Guilty' and, at the same time, hammer home mitigating circumstances which, in turn, might effect Belmont's idea of an appropriate sentence when the jury returned their verdict.

The required legal rigmarole had been gone through; the jury were in place, Belmont was seated, with open notebook and ballpoint at the ready, Blayde was in the witness box waiting. I'd already noted that Blayde's face looked grey and a little drawn as if he, too, had had a sleepless night. It might help. At least, it evened things up a little. I, too, had had a restless night.

Before I could rise, Clipstone was on his feet.

He said, 'M'lord, before the cross-examination of the witness, I wish to ask the court's indulgence.'

Belmont showed ill-tempered interest.

'My third police witness,' said Clipstone. 'Chief Superintendent Tallboy. Matters of some urgency — matters of a private nature — force me to request that his evidence be dispensed with.'

'M'lord ...'

Belmont waved me silent, then asked, 'Important evidence?'

'Evidence ...' Clipstone seemed to choose his words with great care. 'Evidence of an *obiter dicta* nature in the main.'

'Whitehouse?' Belmont turned his attention to me.

Before I could reply, Clipstone said, 'M'lord, the Prosecution has no objection to the Defence using the deposition given at the committal proceedings by Chief Superintendent Tallboy as a basis for the additional cross-examination of this witness.'

'Hearsay evidence?' grunted Belmont.

'It need not be, m'lord. Much — indeed *most* — of what Chief Superintendent Tallboy knows is also known by the present witness.'

'In that case . . .'

'If the court will allow some small relaxation of the rules of evidence, m'lord. The Prosecustion has no objection.' Clipstone smiled. 'The duration of the case might be shortened.'

Belmont nodded, a little ponderously. Never have I known a judge so eager to rush a case — *any* case — to its conclusion.

He said, 'You make this in the form of an application, Mr Clipstone?'

'I do, m'lord.'

'I will record it as such.' Belmont turned to me and murmured, 'Mr Whitehouse?'

'As your lordship pleases.'

As I stooped — on the face of it to sort through my papers, but in fact to consider this latest twist of the case — from behind me Armstrong whispered, 'It's a trick, sir.'

'I doubt it,' I breathed. 'Clipstone doesn't conduct his cases that way.'

'It *could* be a ploy,' murmured Smith-Hopkinson.

'Keep your wits about you.' I shuffled Tallboy's deposition, and continued to speak in a whisper. 'If I miss anything, let me know.' Then I straightened, smiled at Belmont, bobbed my head, turned to the witness box and said, 'When you're ready, chief superintendent.'

'When you are, sir.'

'Right.' I nodded. 'Can we start by accepting the fact that the murdered woman's name was Helena Schnitzler?'

'Yes, sir.'

'That she was *not* a Jewess?'

'She wasn't a Jewess, sir.'

'That far from being a Jewess . . .' Something — some sixth sense — urged me to ask the dangerous question. 'Far from being a Jewess, she was a wardress at Belsen concentration camp.'

In a very steady voice Blayde said, 'I have that on very good authority, sir.'

'What authority?' Belmont asked the question.

'My lord.' Blayde turned slightly, in order to face Belmont. 'As I said in the evidence-in-chief, the accused voluntarily gave himself into my custody on Wednesday, October 29th. That was when I was told — by the accused — that the dead woman's name *was* Helena Schnitzler, and that she'd been a wardress at Belsen. Since that date I've made careful enquiries. I can state, on oath, that as far as I can ascertain that *was* her name and that *was* her one-time employment.'

'To your satisfaction?' pressed Belmont.

'To my complete satisfaction, my lord.'

'Thank you, chief superintendent.' Belmont moved the hand not holding the pen. 'Please continue, Mr Whitehouse.'

'Chief superintendent,' I began, 'can we go back to that interview? The interview with the accused on Wednesday, October 29th?'

'Yes, sir.'

'Now . . .' I phrased my question with great care. 'Throughout that interview — at any time during that interview — did the accused specifically, and in as many words, admit to being the murderer of Helena Schnitzler?'

'No, sir. He did not.'

'Did he deny murdering her?'

'Yes, sir. I asked him a direct question after administering the caution. I said, "Did you kill Annie Miller?" His reply was "No".'

'Annie Miller?'

'At that time, and as far as the police were concerned, that was the name of the dead woman.'

Something passed between us. What it was is hard to define. I know Blayde's eyes widened fractionally; as if warning me not to continue this line of questioning. I know I trusted him and accepted the warning. The trial had suddenly taken upon itself a strange, Alice-in-Wonderland quality. *Blayde was on our side!* The modern generation uses the term 'vibes' . . . presumably meaning vibrations. I knew what the term meant. ESP if you like. Whatever, it was there. I glanced at Clipstone and saw him bent forward over his notes; deliberately — or so it seemed — cutting himself off from the cross-examination; content to allow the case to slip from his grasp, without objection. I turned my head and looked at Gold in the dock. He stood rigid with an expressionless face; as if he, too, had divorced himself from the court proceedings and was waiting for . . .

For *what*?

Belmont cleared his throat pointedly.

'M'lord,' I apologised. Then to Blayde, 'You — er — you saw the dead woman? Before she was removed?'

'I did.'

'That — er — that piano wire?' I pointed to one of the Prosecution exhibits.

'The piano wire on which she died.' It sounded like an echo, and I realised that Blayde was deliberately quoting the words used by Gold during the interrogation.

I moved a hand, and a court usher handed the exhibit to Blayde. Blayde held it in his left hand. Smith-Hopkinson handed me a second length of piano wire. I handed it to the usher and Blayde accepted it in his right hand.

I said, 'The wire I've just handed you, chief superintendent. It was purchased at Lessford.'

'Yes, sir.' Blayde glanced down at the two lengths of wire.

'Similar?' I suggested.

'I can see no difference, sir.'

'Gold — the accused — purchased the second length of wire at my direction.'

'Yes, sir.'

'A receipt was given.'

'Yes, sir.'

Again the usher handed the Lessford receipt to Blayde.

'The exhibit please.'

The usher took the receipt given to Gold, and handed it to Blayde. I said, 'Both receipts for piano wire?'

'Yes, sir.'

'Different dates, of course?'

'Yes, sir.'

'One from Lessford. One from London.'

'Yes, sir.'

'To whom were those receipts given, chief superintendent?'

'Sir, I'm on oath,' said Blayde in a low voice.

'Let me phrase it differently. To whom do you *think* those two receipts were given?'

'I've been told they were both given to the accused.'

'Told?'

'You've just told me, sir.' Blayde raised the second receipt slightly. 'The London receipt. Gold told me. Enquiries have been made. The receipt is from that firm, but the accused isn't known to that firm. Nor do they recognise a photograph of Gold.'

'The receipts are signed, of course?'

'Yes, sir.'

'Dated?'

'Yes, sir.'

'And made out to whom?'

'It doesn't say, sir. It doesn't say on either receipt.'

'Therefore . . . to *anybody*?'

'To anybody, sir.'

'Thank you, superintendent.'

'*Chief* superintendent,' murmured Belmont.

'My apologies, my lord.' I smiled at Blayde. 'Thank you *chief* superintendent.'

The usher stepped forward, took the receipts and the wire from Blayde, and returned them to the table. Blayde waited. The impression was that he had reached a decision and, having reached it, had infinite patience. I've never seen a bullfight (nor indeed want to) but from what I have read — from what I have heard — there comes a point at which a magnificent animal accepts its fate; when it has done what it was bred to do, when it has been goaded to fury by the picadors and when, despite its courage and strength, it is forced to acknowledge the simple fact of defeat. It is known as 'The Moment of Truth', and the bull — still proud, still undefeated in spirit — awaits the sword of the espada. Blayde reminded me of such a moment. He dominated the whole court . . . yet waited, patiently, for me to destroy him.

I leaned forward a little, opened the box in which near-priceless jewellery caught what little light the court room contained and turned that light into tiny sparks of fire.

I said, 'This box. It was found buried in the back garden of the dead woman's home?'

'It was.'

'Found by Chief Superintendent Tallboy, but you are in a position to verify the facts of its finding on oath?'

'I am, sir.'

'Has any attempt been made to value its contents, chief superintendent?'

'We've tried, sir.' He sighed and gave a quick smile. 'None of the experts are prepared to give even an approximate value.'

'Priceless?' I suggested.

'That term has been used, sir . . . often.'

'What enquiries have been made concerning the contents?' I asked.

'It's not . . .' He paused, then started again. 'Extensive – very extensive – enquiries have been made, sir. Each item has been photographed and circulated. Nationally. Even internationally, and that, sir, includes a circulation, as far as has been possible, behind the Iron Curtain. That has been the extent of the circulation of the jewellery. None of it is recorded as having been stolen. Not one item.'

'Not stolen property?' I murmured.

'I – er – I didn't say that, sir.'

I raised questioning eyebrows . . . and hoped. My hopes were realised.

Blayde said, 'Certain presumptions must be made, sir. If, as I believe, Schnitzler was a wardress at Belsen concentration camp, it can be presumed that the jewellery *was* stolen. From the inmates. From prisoners . . .' He paused, moistened his lips, then ended, 'From prisoners, perhaps for small mercies, or prior to them being herded into the gas chambers.'

To say that I 'won' the case . . .

It would be untrue. I am credited with victory, but it is untrue. Blayde *gave* the case to me. More than that even. Clipstone sat at one side, and *allowed* Blayde to present me with the case. Belmont couldn't understand it. Nor more could I. Twice in the course of my lengthy cross-examination he held up a silencing hand and said,

'Mr Clipstone?' Each time Clipstone raised his head, smiled and gave a tiny shake of the head. Each time Belmont looked surprised, then murmured, 'Please continue, Mr Whitehouse.'

Nor did the strangeness end there. Of all of the participants in the trial Gold, the accused man, seemed least important. Towards the end the impression was that it wasn't Gold who was on trial . . . it was the dead woman, Helena Schnitzler. Not what she was, but what she'd once *been*.

A most peculiar case. A case (and of this I had no doubt) to be argued over countless times in the future, while enjoying good port and fine cigars in every Inn of Court.

As I sat down, Smith-Hopkinson breathed, 'That's *it*, sir.'

It was indeed 'it'.

Clipstone rose, bowed to the judge and said, 'With the court's permission, m'lord. I wish to make formal request for the record to read *nolle prosequi* at this point.'

'Agreed.' Belmont frowned, then continued, 'In turn, I am curious to know why this case was brought to this court in the first place.'

'There seemed a case to answer, m'lord,' drawled Clipstone.

'Indeed?'

'We thought so, m'lord.'

' "We"?'

'The police, m'lord, having been advised by counsel.'

'By you?'

'By the D.P.P., m'lord.' Clipstone sighed. 'I must, of course, accept responsibility on behalf of that office.'

'Indeed you must.' Belmont's voice reminded me of the threatening rumblings of a volcano. 'At the same time, you will note my displeasure – my *extreme* displeasure – at this outrageous waste of valuable time. You will convey that displeasure to the chief constable responsible for so wasting valuable court time and, with my compliments, suggest that in future he evaluates the evidence and possible conviction of an accused person with more care.'

'M'lord.'

The jury were dismissed, with profuse apologies for the gross stupidity of the Prosecution in general and the police in particular.

Gold had his freedom restored to him with a somewhat lofty wave of the hand and no apology at all. Armstrong, Smith-Hopkinson and I collected up our papers and followed Clipstone and his junior from the court.

In the robing room as we packed away our wigs, bibs and gowns, Clipstone gave me a slightly watery smile.

'What is known as being judicially emasculated,' he murmured.

'It happens, but we survive.'

We were alone in one corner — beyond earshot of our juniors — and in a strange voice, he said, 'Accepting the complete unreliability of any jury, do you think you'd have won?'

'We *did* win.' I stared at him uncomprehendingly.

'Come now, Whitehouse. You were allowed to win.'

'I'm sorry, Clipstone, I don't follow your . . .'

'Blayde handed you the case on a platter.'

'He was a poor witness,' I conceded.

'He's a detective chief superintendent.'

'My dear Clipstone, I've known detective chief superintendents . . .'

'Not of his calibre.'

'Are you seriously suggesting . . .'

'Nothing, my dear chap.' He pulled the draw-strings of his scarlet bag and strolled from the room.

I took my time dressing and, when I left the robing room, I deliberately walked along corridors where I knew neither Armstrong nor Smith-Hopkinson might be. Outside the building, I hailed a cab and asked to be taken to Bordfield Regional Police Headquarters.

I identified myself to a sergeant who answered my ring at the police counter, and was told that Chief Superintendent Blayde had not yet arrived back from court. I asked to be allowed to wait and the sergeant led me up to the second floor to Blayde's office, and there I settled in one of the moderately comfortable chairs.

About twenty minutes later Blayde joined me. He seemed only mildly surprised at my visit; as if he'd been half-expecting me to call on him. We exchanged greetings, I offered cigarettes then, when we were smoking, he moved to the swivel-chair behind the desk and waited.

'You lost the case.' I saw no point in beating about the bush.

He moved one shoulder resignedly.

'Deliberately,' I amplified.

A gentle but slightly mischievous smile touched his lips as he said, 'On paper it's 'Detected'. Beyond that it's no concern of the police.'

'You deliberately lost the case,' I insisted. 'You. Personally. You *gave* it to me.'

'You think Gold deserved prison?' he asked mockingly.

'Chief superintendent, I'm a Queen's Counsel, I . . .'

'I'm *not*.'

'No.' I suddenly realised how impossibly pompous I must have sounded. I drew on the cigarette then in a quieter, more modified tone said, 'I'd like to know. I'd like to think you trust me.'

'Four walls?' He moved his head pointedly.

'Not beyond,' I said. 'You have my word.'

He tapped ash into an ash-tray as he began, 'Clipstone and I know each other. Not well. Not buddy-buddy. But enough to ask favours occasionally. I asked him not to 'object'. He agreed.'

'And Chief Superintendent Tallboy. Was he . . .'

'He'll be well again — back in his office at Beechwood Brook — tomorrow.'

I nodded my head slowly, then murmured, 'The *nolle prosequi*?'

'Clipstone's idea.' He almost grinned. 'What else?'

'Belmont wasn't amused.'

'Judges.' He raised his eyes and gazed with mock-interest at the ceiling of the office. 'They know all about law . . . damn-all about justice.'

'Nevertheless . . .'

'I'll get a quick ballocking from on high.' He gave a little nod towards the ceiling, as if to indicate what he meant from the words 'on high', then continued, 'Part of the job, Mr Whitehouse. It'll be given. It'll be received. Then forgotten. No hard feelings on either side.' He lowered his gaze. 'Something else judges don't understand. Unknown in *their* rarified atmosphere.'

'As easy as that?' I said quietly.

'As easy as *that*.' He gazed at me for a moment — much as a worldly-wise adult might gaze at a slow-witted child — then, in a voice tinged with harshness, said, 'We have to make it *work*, Mr Whitehouse. All those fancy theories. The Acts of Parliament. The Case Law. The high-sounding legal crap published in all the expensive textbooks. We have to take it onto the street and, by fair means or foul, make the bloody stuff work. Which means we have to bend it round corners. Stretch it a little. Compress it a little. It's not easy . . . sometimes it's bloody impossible. Nevertheless we do it, because we're paid to do it. We wheel and deal a little. We horse-trade. We conveniently 'forget' things. Ours is not an 'academic' job, sir. It's a very *practical* job, but the damn academics are forever telling us how to do it.' He drew on the cigarette. A quick, deep draw, as if the anger inside him needed extra draught in order to bring it up to the required temperature. 'You — not you, personally, but your kind — work like hell to shackle us. 'Innocent until proved guilty', when we *know* he couldn't be more guilty if he was Old Nick himself. And the other kind. Like Gold. Every card in the deck stacked against him, but morally he's a new-born babe.'

'Judge. Jury. Executioner,' I mused.

'That's us,' he growled. 'Be grateful we've accepted the triple role. It's a hell of a sight more than we're paid for. Let me give you the truth.' He used the two fingers holding the cigarette to stab the accusation home at me. 'You people. Barristers, solicitors, lecturers in law . . . men who don't have to *practise* the law. Not talk about it — talk around it — argue it up, down, sideways, every direction under the sun . . . *practise* it. You want the truth? As you preach it, it won't work. Not in a thousand years. Pure law is pure hogwash. Like perpetual motion. On paper? — in the lecture room? — fine. Out on the streets? — no way. No bloody *way*! It needs a push. Sometimes it needs one hell of a shove. That's our job.' He paused, then in a quieter tone said, 'You came here to ask why. *That's* why.'

'I'm — I'm sorry,' I said, clumsily. And I *was* sorry although for the life of me I couldn't put my finger on *why* I was sorry.

'It's okay. It's part of the service.' The twisted grin softened his features. The eyes lost their flint-like anger. As he stood up from the desk to open the office door for me he said, 'We've handed the civil lib lunatics a banner. That's what gripes. Poor, inoffensive Jew. And a bitch like Schnitzler. And we tried to fit him up for *her* murder. That's how they'll see it. The police . . . not the law. Tomorrow's headlines. Bet your life on it. You'll be a hero.'

We shook hands and I left.

THREE

On the train back to London I didn't feel like a hero. I felt . . .

'Unclean' would be too strong a word. And yet part of it *was* moving in that direction. I certainly felt dismayed. I'd accepted the brief, knowing that I'd be defending a guilty man. That, of itself, smacked of shysterism. I'd identified myself with the 'cause' which had tracked down Helena Schnitzler and, because of that personal identification, I'd been prepared to turn a life-long principle inside out.

The great advocates — Marshall Hall, Hastings, Russell, Erskine, Rufus Isaacs, Birkett — had they ever shelved their consciences? Had they ever known — *known* for a proven fact — that the man or woman they'd been defending was guilty? Probably suspected — possibly even more than suspected — but that wasn't the same thing. An advocate's job, indeed an advocate's duty, is to present his client's case in as good a manner as he is able; he — long before the jury is sworn — must grant to his client reasonable and, sometimes, *un*reasonable doubt. The benefit of *all* doubt.

But had any of the giants ever *known*?

Smith-Hopkinson felt — probably saw from my expression — the darkness of my mood. We shared the table in the buffet car for lunch and, being young and somewhat impetuous, he could contain his curiosity no longer.

'Something's troubling you, sir,' he remarked.

'Courts of law. Courts of justice,' I sighed.

'I'm sorry.' He looked puzzled.

'What would *you* call them?' I asked.

'Courts of . . . law?' He raised his voice at the end, and made it a question.

'I'm inclined to agree,' I said morosely. 'Courts of law . . . in which justice is sometimes meted out.'

'More than occasionally, sir. Surely?'

'Perhaps. But what if in order to obtain justice — what *we* believe to be justice — we subscribe to the upturning of the law?'

'Justice,' he said with a smile. 'Equity . . . as in R.v.Gold.'

'Criminal Law?' I pressed quickly.

'I know.' He nodded, forked food into his mouth, chewed, swallowed then continued. 'Crown Courts. Originally Queen's Bench Division, Assize, Oyer and Terminer and all the rest of it. Equity — Jurisprudence — doesn't mix with Criminal Law. But it damn well *should*. I've known some God-awful decisions in criminal courts. Obviously, so have you. What we've just done? Prevent one more.'

'So easy,' I sighed. 'To the youth, so clear. So cut and dried.'

'Sir.' He hesitated and, for Smith-Hopkinson, the expression and the words were uncommonly sombre. 'Back in chambers I've listened to arguments. Not from you . . . I've always looked upon you as *not* one of the nit-pickers. But those everlasting arguments. Never black, never white, always grey. Grey, uninteresting and completely non-productive. Perhaps, as a barrister, I shouldn't entertain such thoughts, but to me it *is* simple. There's right and there's wrong. And often circumstances determine the difference. Murder . . . it's *not* just the killing. The gradations are infinite. Every man, every woman . . . external pressures can cause them to kill. Everybody! And to squeeze all that into a single box and label it 'Murder' . . . it's ridiculous. More than that, it's unjust. Schnitzler was killed. If she hadn't ducked from under, she'd have gone with Grese. The hangman would have killed them both. As far as I'm concerned, she's stolen a lifetime she didn't deserve. Gold took from her something that wasn't hers in the first place.'

'Ah, but did he have the right?'

'If not him, who? Albert Pierrepoint? Because *he* wore British Army uniform? Because other men in uniform had been told what we already know? Helena Schnitzler was Helena Schnitzler — complete with every last abomination she committed against helpless people — and nothing on God's earth will ever change that. Not even the way she died.'

'So sure,' I murmured sadly. 'So sure. You . . . and another man with an equally uncomplicated view of right and wrong.'

VICTIM

ONE

Sachsenhausen was not one of the big camps. Not an important camp. Not like Dachau. Not like Buchenwald. Sachsenhousen was merely one of the more than three hundred lesser camps; one of the smaller cogs in the great machine of genocide.

In such a camp it was possible to survive. Not to live, you understand — not to enjoy oneself, to laugh, to play, to relax — but to clamp the teeth hard upon the need to exist, and thus to survive. It meant learning the tricks . . . and quickly. It meant lying and stealing. It meant forgetting dignity, forgetting pride, forgetting even simple humanity. To survive meant accepting filth and foulness. It meant forcing an empty stomach to accept — even to embrace — food unfit for pigs. It meant accepting death — disgusting death — as a daily, almost hourly, occurrence.

It was possible to survive.

The pain? The disease? The humiliation? Trivialities. Pain, disease and humiliation were part of civilisation and the camps were islands wherein civilisation did not run. Pain could be tolerated; it never became a friend, but over the months and years it became a companion. Pain was merely . . . pain. To feel pain was proof that one still survived, therefore pain was a yardstick. Pain was a proof. It wasn't a nightmare, it was real and the evidence that it was real was the pain and the beatings which brought on the pain. Pain meant you were surviving, therefore pain was almost welcomed. As with disease. A corpse could suffer no disease, *ergo* disease meant you were not yet a corpse. Survival was still possible. Disease was proof of that possibility. As for humiliation . . . what *was* humiliation? The rags, the dirt, the cold, the hunger? There was a threshold. Beyond that threshold the word 'humiliation' had no meaning. The warders and the wardresses 'made fun'. That was the expression they used. They 'made fun'. But the 'fun' was finite. Imagination — even perverted imagination — had a limit. The body — the human body — could be subjected to only so much 'fun'. Thereafter it became boring rather than humiliating. To survive it . . . that was the thing. To survive the 'fun'. To survive *everything*.

The rabbi visited the women's part of the camp at Sachsenhausen once each week. He came from the men's camp. He came to give comfort . . . to remind them that they were God's chosen people. The rabbi; many different rabbis. A rabbi was, by definition, a Jew. Because he was a rabbi — because he was a Jew — his life could be counted in days, weeks — months at the most. And the women who sought comfort? They also, by definition, were Jewish. It was dangerous to seek comfort. It was wise *not* to join the women who sought comfort.

It was wise to survive!

Sometimes — often — the rabbi was hauled forward to be an unwilling participant when they 'made fun'. Again, at such times, it was wise to smile. To obediently laugh at degradation. To participate, should a warden or a wardress push you forward as a chosen player in these games of foulness and inhumanity. To participate . . . to survive. To smile . . . to survive. To indulge in mock-laughter . . . to survive.

Always . . . *to survive*.

Once — only once — one of the holy men had cornered her in an angle of one of the huts. He'd argued. He'd pleaded.

'My child, you must trust in God.'

'God!' Quite deliberately she'd spat on the filthy boards.

'We are His children.'

'Go outside,' she'd taunted. 'Teach *them*. Convince *them*.'

'He is great, my child. He can comfort. He can . . .'

She'd raked his face with her broken fingernails. The beard had saved the lower half of his face, but she'd aimed for the eyes. The blood had run. It had soaked into, then dripped off, the beard. Streaks of shiny scarlet down the front of the stained prison jacket. Drops falling and soaking into the grime of the floor.

She'd screamed, 'Christ killer!' then dodged round him and run panting from the hut.

The secret, you see. The secret to be quickly learned. To be what 'they' said you were. A thing without a soul; without a conscience, without honour, without self-respect. To accept the indignities as being all you were fit for. To be penned like a beast with other beasts within the confines of wire. To forget you were a human being — that you'd ever *been* a human being — to work until your back felt as if it would break, to be forever hungry, to accept the blows and the kicks as just recompense for what you were and for what you'd once, mistakenly, thought yourself to be. To be one tiny spark of life, unloved and without love . . . but, whatever the cost, to guard that spark as the only thing of importance in a whole universe of shame.

TWO

By 1944 the Thousand Year Reich was tumbling. From west and east the great armies were caught within the jaws of avenging and liberating forces. Men to whom had been entrusted The Final Solution grew worried. As the jaws closed camps were being discovered; whispers of hell were reaching the outside world. There was much slaughter, much gassing, much burning, much burying, but it was difficult to remove all evidence in time.

The camps on the perimeter were emptied and cleaned. In cattle trucks, by rail and by road, the inmates were transported farther into Germany — to other and safer camps — while warders and wardresses worked the clock round in an effort to clean and destroy evidence. A mammoth task. An impossible task. But orders had been given, and orders must be obeyed.

And still the jaws closed, and more and more camps had to be emptied. The sub-humans were moved and moved again; always further inland; always to some more 'efficient' camp; nearer and nearer to *the* camp. Like the spokes of a twisted wheel whose hub was Belsen.

The camp at Sachsenhausen earned itself small infamy. The trucks and the rail waggons were not available, therefore they marched.

'The March of Death' it was called. Contemporary historians with a flair for phrase-making called it 'The March of Death'. But there was more than one such march. It was impossible to force the prisoners forward, other than in comparatively small groups — a few hundred at a time — without risking their escape. And they must not be allowed to escape. They must be allowed to die first.

It wasn't too difficult. Dogs, whips, bludgeons, starvation . . . it wasn't *too* difficult.

Hannah Muller was on the third 'march'. March! What a stupid description. They staggered, they fell, they were harried by dogs, they were beaten to their feet again. They were allowed to stop only when they died and, if they fell and were unable to regain their feet, they were shot. Only the living — and *all* the living — reached Belsen.

She ate grass on the way. She chewed the bark of trees. She refused to die. She reduced life to a simple one-plus-one-makes-two proposition. Move the right leg forward. Move the left leg forward. Move the right leg forward. The spark was kept burning, literally, step at a time. The dogs snapped at her heels, but what matter? She'd felt fangs in her flesh many times. The warders and wardresses screamed and cursed, whipped and swung their clubs, but what matter? Pain was the evidence she sought.

Luneburg Forest. She recognised it. She laughed; hysterical cackling, forced from behind rotting and broken teeth, past split lips. Luneburg Forest. She was coming home!

Luneburg Forest . . . within which was Belsen.

Hauptsturmfuhrer Kramer, Camp Commandant at Belsen, worried a little. He was a good German, a good Nazi and he knew how to obey orders . . . but *what* orders! Until recently — until a few months ago — his camp had functioned with clockwork precision. The input and the output had balanced perfectly. The gas chambers and the crematoria disposed of the lower orders with great efficiency. Superb efficiency. Indeed, he doubted whether Himmler could point to another camp whose efficiency equalled that of Belsen. The camp had been built to hold eight thousand, thereabouts. And as that number had lowered a new intake had arrived. A sort of 'topping-up' process. Very civilised. Very orderly. Like a smoothly-running sausage machine; in at one end, out at the other; from scum to smoke, with ashes, old clothing, spectacle frames, rings, gold teeth — many things — as a by-product.

Belsen had been a model camp. Had *all* camps been as smoothly run as Belsen, The Final Solution would have been achieved years before.

It was, perhaps, a mistake to be too efficient. As with all things, efficiency tended to attract attention . . . sometimes unwanted attention.

Eight thousand — a little cramped, perhaps, but they wouldn't be cramped for long — but how in God's name could he be expected to handle more than a hundred thousand? And that at a low estimate. A hundred thousand living, plus at least ten thousand unburied dead. It was monstrous. It was asking too much . . . much too much. They would die — of course they would die, of starvation if of nothing else, and that was the object of the exercise — but what of his staff? What of the warders and the wardresses? Great heaps of bodies in various stages of decomposition. There was a serious health threat. Already two of his warders were in sick quarters, suspected typhus. And it could spread.

'We can't take any more,' he complained to his second-in-command.

'And if they arrive?'

'We can't send them away. That would be to disobey orders from Berlin itself.'

The second-in-command waited. Kramer was the commandant, therefore the problem was Kramer's. The problem seemed to have no solution, therefore he was glad he was not Kramer.

'Bury the dead,' groaned Kramer. 'The chambers — the ovens — they can't handle the load. They have a capacity. They need periodic overhaul. The only answer . . . bury them.'

'The British are not too far away,' observed the second-in-command.

'They will be held.' Kramer hoped he sounded confident. Even at this late stage — even though every right-thinking man knew that defeat was both soon and inevitable — it was wise to keep such opinions unspoken.

The second-in-command said, 'When — *if* — the British arrive it will be their problem.'

'Meanwhile . . . bury them. Make them bury their own dead. The exercise will keep them warm.'

The officer's name was Sington; head of a Psychological Warfare Unit and attached to the British Second Army. A very civilised man and educated at Wellington and Trinity College, Oxford. He'd already heard of concentration camps — sketchy descriptions brought out of occupied Europe by fleeing Jews and, in the main, accepted as more than a little exaggerated in their description by men and women terrified and out to impress. Sington — like the rest of the British Army — was not yet aware of the concentration camp *system*; the careful dovetailing of more than three hundred camps, and the factory-like capacity to hold, then destroy, millions of men and women whose so-called 'purity' was in doubt. Indeed, until that day, he might have scoffed at the suggestion that any nation (even a nation led by a madman and his intimates) could have thought up and perfected such a system.

He'd landed at Normandy on D-Day plus twenty-nine. He'd moved with the advancing British Army through France, through Belgium, through Holland. He'd even seen one of the abandoned camps; the one at Vught which had housed Dutch Jews. He'd seen it, seen the gallows, but still had not comprehended. Why should he? Why should *anybody*? To the civilised world, which Sington and his colleagues took for granted, it was a scenario for a wildly impossible horror film.

Impossible . . . until he saw Belsen.

Nobody fought for Belsen. Nobody died for it. It wasn't even 'captured'. It was handed over after very limited negotiations between senior officers of the British and the German armies. It was dangerous — deadly — in that, within its wire, a typhus epidemic was raging. Let there be a battle, let the war machines of either side breach the wire, and the whole countryside, including soldiers from both armies, would be infected.

So, let the German forces withdraw beyond the camp, and let the camp be handed over to the British. A 'gentleman's agreement' . . .

and Sington was the first British officer to enter. To see. To believe. To be *made* to believe.

Kramer knew how to behave in such circumstances. It was possible to be dignified, even in defeat. It was possible to impress. The SS officers — the warders and wardresses — stood in ranks before the main gate. They stood to attention as the car braked to a halt and Kramer saluted Sington as Sington climbed from the car. Certain introductions were made — politenesses were performed — and still Sington didn't realise. He hadn't yet *seen*. The front compound — the area immediately beyond the gate — was taken up by office blocks and stores. The nightmare was beyond that first compound.

'For the moment they are subdued.' Kramer's voice was friendly; as friendly as a farmer explaining the volatility of his livestock. 'You should take care. They may become excited.'

That, at least — Kramer knew his prisoners.

Kramer stood on the running board as Sington drove slowly into the main compounds; saw the ten thousand unburied dead piled in twisted mountains of contorted bodies; saw the mass graves, each holding forty thousand corpses; saw the not-yet-dead as they surged towards the car, and saw the dozens who died (that day of all days) as the guards opened fire in an attempt to quell the stampede.

Poor Sington. He gave evidence at the War Crimes Trial. He wrote books about it. As a fine peacetime journalist he had a way with words, but what he saw that day was beyond mere words. It beggared description. It had to be seen to be believed.

Certainly it was something beyond the normal scope of even the British Army. Inside the camp typhus raged and had to be contained. Prisoners and jailers alike had to remain within the wire until the epidemic was tamed. The warders and wardresses were given the task of burying the forty thousand dead. The soldiers stood guard as best they could, but to the determined there was a score of escape routes where a British Tommy would turn his back on some ragged inmate fleeing this disease-ridden charnel-house.

THREE

But *she'd* seen it. 'Annie Miller' had seen it. She'd been part of it. A lifetime ago . . . but yesterday. Wherever she looked, whatever she saw, the scenes were superimposed upon her vision. The stench had never left her nostrils. The screams had never left her ears.

She trembled. She might have had palsy, such was her trembling, as she lowered herself onto the chair and re-read the note.

> *Helena Schnitzler,*
> *Be at home.   Three rings.   We find*
> *you now. We will find you again.*
>   *'H'*

Plain but not cheap paper. Folded and slipped into one of her shopping bags while she'd been out at Beechwood Brook. It could have been anybody. Any of a hundred people. Man or woman, she'd no idea. When or where, there was no means of knowing. Just that 'they' had traced her. That she *still* wasn't safe.

Today was Monday. Monday, October 13th, and today they knew her. Knew what she looked like. Knew how she dressed. Knew where she shopped. Knew where she lived. Knew everything.

An old woman, but still running.

She knew what the 'H' meant. The Hunter. An organisation; a small organisation but (or so it seemed) with limitless powers. With a bottomless purse. With patience which never slackened. She'd heard rumours — sometimes more than rumours — and always The Hunter finally reached out and pinned the prey. The Hunter. One of a dozen or more similar groups. Searching . . . forever searching. Never saying 'Enough!' For how long? In God's name, for how long? 'Vengeance is mine; I will repay, saith the Lord'. But how *much* vengeance? And for how long? For ever? Was there *never* to be rest?

To be hunted . . . but *why* was she hunted? Why had she *allowed* herself to be hunted? Why had she built up a pretence which to her had gradually become more real than reality?

The camps. Blame it all on the camps. Blame it all on a system which had made her deny her God; which had allowed her to accept a fortune filched from the condemned of her own kind. Which had perhaps driven her a little crazy; crazy enough to run because she'd shamed a name which had once been the only shred of pride she could still lay claim to.

Over the years they'd hounded her. The Hunter. Other groups. May she rot in hell if they hadn't hounded her. May she rot in hell if she hadn't paid the price. From Germany through war-torn Europe. West to Holland, south to Belgium. South again to France, then east to Switzerland. Taking her tiny casket of wealth with her; smuggling it past border posts; seeking out buyers prepared to purchase but not ask too many questions. At first the box had been full. It had been difficult to close the lid. But now . . .

Seven years she'd stayed in Switzerland. Small hotels. Nothing too expensive. Comfort. Oh, yes, comfort of a sort. But not luxury. How long had she to live? How many years? And the jewel casket had to last. Therefore quietly. Not in luxury. Not making friends. Not even allowing the hotel staff pleasant familiarity.

Seven years . . . then on the move again. Some sixth sense had warned her. Tiny things. A man staring into a shop window, but *not* staring into a shop window. Then the same man, but another shop window. Tiny things, but the antennae of the hunted had picked them up.

West again to France. Zig-zagging across France; Nantes, Lyon, Bordeaux, then north to Le Havre. Then across the English Channel. More hotels; tiny hotels, boarding houses. Sidmouth, then east to Yarmouth; into Wales to Aberdovey; a spell in the Black Country, then into Lincolnshire, to Louth; then north to Leeds, to Harrogate, to Bradford . . . and, finally, here. Her own house at Rimstone.

May she rot in hell if she hadn't paid the price!

Helena Schnitzler,
Be at home. Three rings. We find
you now. We will find you again.
'H'

A tear dripped from the end of her nose and smudged the strong, square-cut writing.

God she was tired. Nobody knew. Nobody could possibly know. Tired of running. Tired of life. Tired of everything.

She pulled a soiled handkerchief from her coat pocket, blew her nose and stopped weeping. She reached into one of the bags and lifted out the bunch of cheap chrysanthemums, then walked into the kitchen. She burned the note in the ash-clogged grate; watching the paper curl and flame until it was completely destroyed. Then she dumped the flowers into the vase on the mahogany sideboard. She didn't change the water. She made no attempt at arrangement. She merely plunged the stalks into the already-smelling water, stood back and looked at the flowers.

She loved flowers, because it was safe to love flowers . . . as easy and as simple as that. She was a woman therefore, by nature, she had to love *something*. An animal? A cat or a dog? It had never been practical; on the run, forever on the move . . . it hadn't been practical. Nor at Rimstone. Animals had to be 'walked' or, at the very least, 'let out' occasionally. They could forge a link; force her to acknowledge the existence of *people*. Neighbours. Other cat- or dog-lovers. The last thing she wanted.

Therefore, flowers. Flowers — even cheap flowers — had a beauty, and her own life hadn't contained much beauty. Other than in flowers, the world was not a beautiful place and, when flowers died and lost their beauty, they could be replaced . . . and nobody would be angry.

She stared at the chrysanthemums for all of five minutes. Noting their bronze and their yellows, the curl of their petals, the dying explosion of their autumn tints.

Then she went about her normal daily chores. She could run no farther. Supposing her life-span could be measured in weeks — even days — no matter . . . she could run no farther.

FOUR

They came on the Thursday. Thursday, October 16th, at about half an hour after midnight . . . the day had just been born. Three rings on the bell-push. Three distinct rings, two distinct pauses. The unhurried deliberation, coupled with the o'clock, left her in no doubt.

They might, perhaps, have given her a little longer. That was her first thought. A little longer to . . .

To *what*?

Like a faulty neon strip, a sad smile flickered at her lips and was gone. To wait? To wonder? To remember? That was all she had left. Memories, and not a good memory amongst them. They were, perhaps, kind not to have prolonged the waiting.

Since receiving the note she hadn't slept in her bed. She'd cat-napped in this armchair. Afraid to go upstairs, afraid to undress and go to bed in case she missed their arrival. It was important — she didn't know why, but it *was* important — that she was not caught unawares. Perhaps it had something to do with dignity . . . she couldn't be sure. A last, final dignity. A means of convincing them that she wasn't afraid. Who knows? Perhaps a means of making *them* ashamed.

She walked to the hall, turned the Yale latch-lock and opened the door and, for the first time, saw them. Two of them. Two men; not of an age; a youngish man, and a man who had years enough to be the younger man's father. Neatly dressed . . . both of them neatly dressed. Including loose-fitting macs, hats and gloves.

The elder man said, 'Helena Schnitzler?'

His voice was quiet and calm. He even raised his hand and lifted his hat a few inches clear of his head in a token gesture of politeness.

She opened the door wide, and they stepped into the hall. She closed the door, and the latch-lock snapped into place. Neither man removed either hat or gloves as they entered the house.

As she led them into the front room, the elder man said, 'You got our note?'

She nodded. For the moment she couldn't trust herself to speak. She wanted no tremor in her voice. She wasn't afraid, and she didn't want to *sound* afraid.

Death? What was death? A prolonged sleep . . . anybody who believed death to be other than that was a fool. And sleep was a friend. Therefore, death was a friend. Only the manner of dying mattered. Not starvation; she'd seen starvation and starvation was slow and degrading. Not the chambers; the chambers, too, she knew . . . the screaming and clawing, and the twisted tortured corpses when the doors were opened.

Not that . . . therefore she wasn't afraid.

'We thought we'd never find you,' sighed the elder man.

'A few more years.' Her voice was steady, and she smiled.

'An injustice,' said the elder man gently.

She continued to smile. There was no humour in the smile. A touch of sadness, perhaps. But in the main a form of silent absolution for what she knew they were there to do.

'You were there?' she asked, and it was a polite question asked in a polite voice.

'Auschwitz.'

'It wasn't like Belsen.'

'*Nowhere* was like Belsen.'

'No,' she agreed.

The younger man was nonplussed. It was beyond him. It made his flesh creep. They were like old friends, reminiscing; comparing experiences of times long past. There was no hatred. No contempt. Instead, there was a twisted form of friendship. Almost a quiet admiration. It was well beyond his understanding. He cleared his throat and took the two lengths of line from a pocket of his mac.

The elder man spoke almost apologetically.

'My colleague is anxious to do what we are here to do.'

'Of course.' She held out her hands.

'Behind your back, please.'

She nodded, obeyed, and the younger man lashed her wrists together behind her back. She offered no resistance.

'A cigarette?' suggested the elder man.

'No, thank you.'

'Anything?'

'Nothing you could give me.' She smiled. 'Nothing you'd be allowed to give me.'

'No,' agreed the elder man sadly. He motioned to the armchair, then held one of her elbows to steady her as she lowered herself. As the younger man began to lash her ankles together, he continued,

'We should have fought. We shouldn't have listened.'

'Listened?'

'The propaganda. We listened, and we really *believed*. We weren't human beings. We were vermin. We weren't fit to live.'

'It's an explanation,' she admitted. 'That . . . or a racial death wish.'

'Just one each,' mused the elder man. His eyes looked into the past and saw all the misery and all the mistakes. 'We knew. Something the world still can't understand . . . we *knew*. The knock on the door. The arrest. The disappearances. We knew where we were going. *We* knew about the camps. Just one each . . . that's all. If each Jew had killed one Nazi. A life for a life . . . no more. Six million. Hitler, minus six million of his followers. He'd have called a halt. He'd have *had* to call a halt.'

'He might.' It was only half-agreement.

'Knowing Hitler,' admitted the elder man sombrely. 'Knowing what he became.'

The younger man went to the hall. When he returned he was holding piano wire in his hands. He'd already fashioned a noose.

'There's a peg in the hall,' he croaked.

'He's afraid.' There was gentle mockery in her voice. She glanced at the younger man, returned her gaze to the elder man and said, 'It's there. It's always there. He's afraid. *Always* afraid. Where's your one-for-one theory now?'

'He's a reluctant executioner. That's all. He doesn't *enjoy* taking life.'

'And you?'

As he helped her from the chair – like an elderly, well-mannered gentleman assisting one of his own generation to her feet – the elder man said, 'We'll see tomorrow's sunrise. That's reward enough.'

They carried her into the hall. The younger man estimated height, then secured one end of the piano wire to a peg. They lifted her and the elder man folded his arms around her knees and held her against the wall while the younger man worked the noose over her head and around her neck. She didn't struggle. She didn't cry out.

The elder man whispered, 'Goodbye, Helena Schnitzler,' and unlocked his arms.

She dropped until her feet were less than twelve inches from the tiled floor. The piano wire bit into her neck, broke a way through the skin and cut off the blood-flow to her brain. It was quick . . . surprisingly quick. There was no need to force herself not to struggle. There was no real time to struggle. Unconsciousness came with the suddenness of a skilfully administered anaesthetic. Unconsciousness . . . then death.

The two men watched, made sure, then let themselves out of the house. They switched off what lights had been lit, closed the door and allowed the latch-lock to click into place. They walked the five hundred yards or so to the parked car, climbed in, then drove back towards Bordfield.

Neither of them spoke.

There was nothing to say . . . or, perhaps, there was too much to say.

EPILOGUE

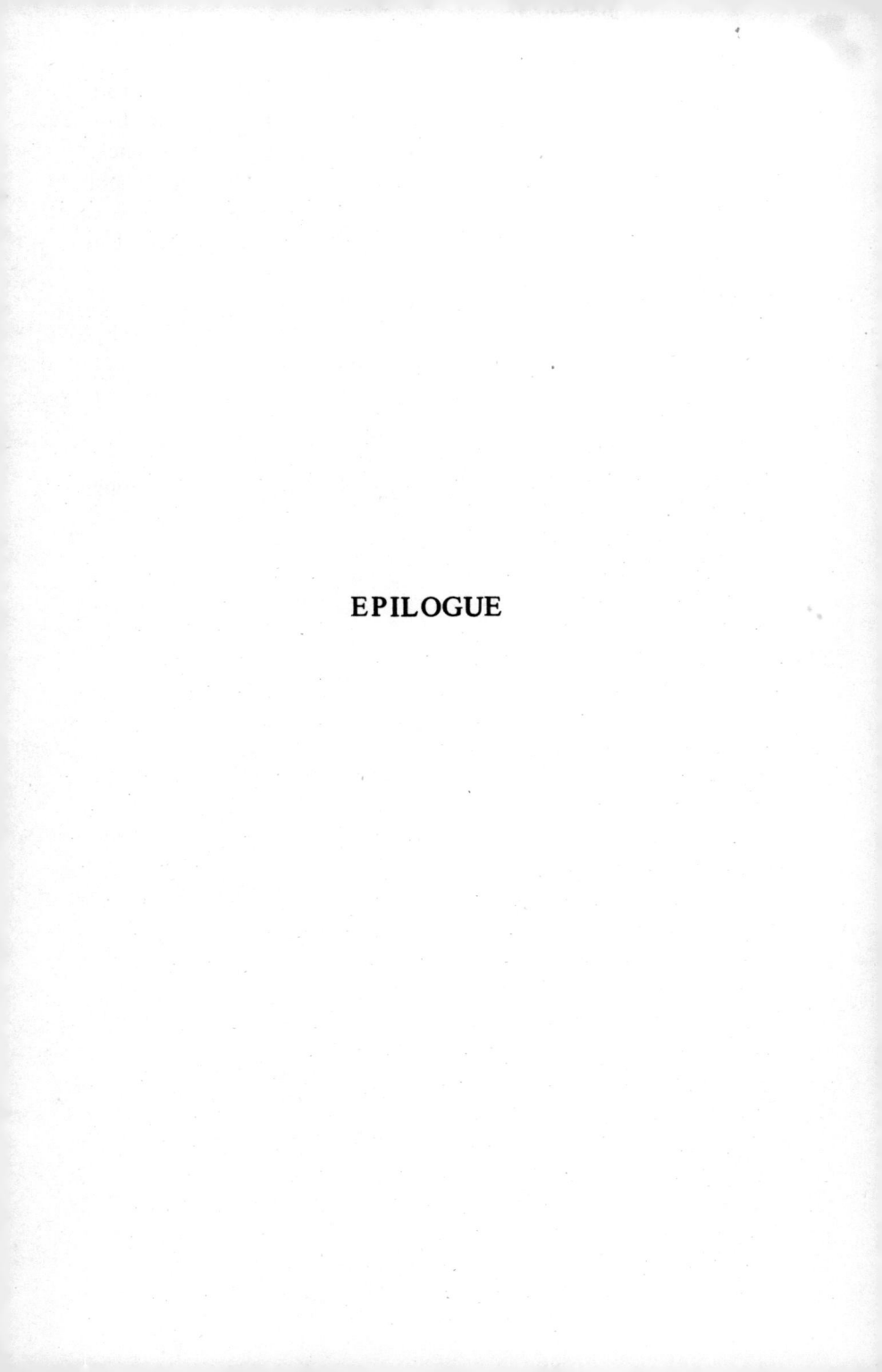

ONE

'Bang goes promotion,' chuckled Tallboy. 'But . . . if you *will* give way to these high-flown principles.'

'*That* . . . from one who never does,' countered Blayde sardonically.

Susan Tallboy looked first at her husband, then at Blayde. Her expression was that usually reserved for exasperated schoolmistresses when confronted by naughty, but beloved, pupils.

'You two,' she proclaimed, 'make a fine pair.'

'Your dad would have been proud of us,' said Tallboy, and, although he smiled, he spoke what he truly believed.

The three of them — Blayde, Tallboy and Susan — were enjoying a pre-Christmas night out. It was Sunday, December 21st and, like all coppers, neither Blayde nor Tallboy could guarantee a quiet and uninterrupted Christmas. Therefore, today being one of the few times when their 'official time off' had coincided, Blayde had suggested a good dinner at one of Bordfield's top restaurants, in order to ensure that at least *one* meal would be remembered of that holiday period. Tallboy had agreed and now, at the coffee-and-brandy stage, the two men were ever so slightly tipsy and allowing their friendship to show more than usual. Susan loved these moments. They were rare but, when they happened, they were well worth the savouring. She had had a light wine with the meal and that was all. When they left the restaurant she would be driving and they'd drop Blayde off at his cottage on their way back to Beechwood Brook.

Meanwhile . . .

'Two of 'em,' grinned Tallboy. 'Poor old Gold was a complete amateur. I checked at the hotel.'

'I know you did.' Blayde raised his glass.

'Two of 'em,' repeated Tallboy. 'Not a clue. Not a bloody clue. They booked in together. They even used their own names.'

'I could . . .' Blayde moved his glass a little to emphasise the point. 'I coulda got old Gold to cough.'

'No doubt of it,' agreed Tallboy solemnly.

'Cough the lot.'

'Anything.'

'Despite Mister Simon Whitehouse, Q.C.'

'That old fuddy-duddy.'

'Why didn't you?' asked Susan innocently.

'Eh?' Blayde stared.

'Why *didn't* you make him cough?'

'My lovely.' Blayde lowered his glass. The impression was that a very sober man was forcing words through the slightly tipsy surface. He said, 'I saw the camps, my pet. I saw . . . places a little like Belsen. Not as bad, but bad enough. I saw people like *her*. I saw what women like Helena Schnitzler could *do*. If they'd done those things to me, I'd have spent the rest of my life tracking 'em down and killing 'em.'

'But, according to Chris, he said . . .'

'He said he'd never been in a camp. He was lying.'

'You're sure?'

'Oh, Susan . . . Susan, Susan, Susan.' Blayde shook his head. 'With your mouth you can lie. But not with your eyes . . . especially about a thing like that. He'd been there. He didn't have to *tell* me.'

'Jewish pride, darling,' explained Tallboy.

'That's one reason – the *only* reason – Gold gave himself up.' Blayde sipped at the brandy. 'Stone's wife opened her stupid trap and Schnitzler – *Schnitzler* of all people – was reported in the news-rags as a Jewess. They had to put the record straight, see? Even if it meant a stretch inside, they couldn't let *that* slide by.'

'But . . .' Tallboy shrugged. 'No more promotion for Bob.'

'Top o' *my* ladder,' agreed Blayde.

'What was the report like?' asked Tallboy.

'Clipstone's?'

'Aye.'

'Very gentle. Y'know . . . very gentle.' Blayde moved his glass again. 'Cut-glass language o' course. And he had to say what Belmont had *told* him to say. But it coulda been a lot worse.'

'And the chief?'

'What are chief constables for?' Blayde's lips twisted into a couldn't-care-a-damn grin. 'A few extra knots in his knickers, but it's what he's paid for. Lemme tell you Chris. I don't wanna go any higher. Where I am . . . that's fine. From here on it's paperwork. Not *bobbying*. I want the streets, old son. I wanna hear the bastards scream when we break their arms. I wanna . . .' He paused, reached for the half-empty bottle of brandy and said, 'I wanna fill-up. How about you?'

'A wise idea.' Tallboy held out his glass. 'Let's get slightly stewed. Let's drink to Gold . . . and what we let him get away with.'

TWO

Christmas Eve. Wednesday, December 24th. It had become an annual occurrence; almost a ritual. Over the years their ranks had changed; the originals had grown fewer in number, but that lessening had been more than compensated for by the introduction of new blood. Therefore, the tankards were raised as high as ever and the songs were roared with as much gusto as in the old days.

Then as the clock eased towards midnight. The stories; stories which over the years had developed into legends.

The lady of the house had just finished telling her story; one of the scores of stories which, in the right company, brought laughter and, sometimes, even applause. She was no fool. She was wise in the ways of sycophants. She knew her wealth — the wealth she had inherited from her dead husband — bought her silence and attention. But, nevertheless, her stories were good stories and well told.

She ended her story and one of her admirers — a young twenty-year-old, with a ramrod back and a neatly trimmed thatch of blond hair — said, 'And she took it?'

'Why not?' The lady of the house laughed. 'Wealth, Fritz, wealth. Before the end of the month we were to be transferred to the civil prison at Celle. Escape from the camp was comparatively easy. Certain with the help of one of the prisoners.'

'So, you sold her your name?'

'No . . . *she* sold me *hers*. On a purely temporary basis, of course.'

'What happened to her?' asked the young man.

'Who knows? Who cares? She helped me escape. After that . . . who knows? Perhaps she, too, escaped. Who knows? She had the means. Some little *hausfrau* somewhere. Forgetting — wishing to forget — where her wealth originated.'

The house stood in its own grounds on the outskirts of Berlin.

The name of the lady of the house was Helena Schnitzler. She'd exchanged that name for the name of her husband — 'on a purely temporary basis, of course' — but on his death, and within the tight security of her chosen friends, she'd reverted back to the name of which she was most proud . . . Helena Schnitzler.

Fiction Wai

Weinstein, John William,

An urge for justice /

Withdrawn

DATE DUE

FEB 24 1983	JUN. 19 1985	OCT 04 1994
APR. 7 1988	MAR 23 1987	NOV 24 1998
APR. 28 1983	OCT 25 1990	
MAY 20 1983	AUG 6 1991	
JUN 3 1983	JAN 6 1992	
AUG. 31 1983	SEP 9 1992	
JUN. 18 1984		
NOV. 8 1984	OCT 06 1993	
JAN 31 1985	OCT 04 1994	
MAY 22 1985		

MHS.

TROY PUBLIC LIBRARY
Troy, New York

3 1182 00993 7805

JAN 4 1982